A Strang

"You snore like a fucking motorboat so I know you're not asleep." She climbed onto the bed, prowling across it to him. "Is this some sick kink? Being a naughty boy for the hot babysitter?"

Her hand squished on the bedspread and she sat up on her knees. "What the hell did you get on my bed, asshole?" She rubbed her fingers and squinted in the darkness at the warm, black goo oozing across them. The bitter aroma of pennies challenged her stomach's hold on her dinner.

The figure rose from the other side of the bed and Piper fell backwards, knocking her head against the floor. She rolled and scurried away as the killer slashed at her legs, scoring the carpet behind her. Piper got her feet under her and shot forward like a sprinter straight into the living room. She unlocked the deadbolt and threw the door open.

The chain-lock caught and the knob slipped out of her hand. She pulled again to the same result. She screamed in frustrated panic. The knife swiped at her again. Her back burned as the skin parted from shoulder to shoulder. Piper turned and begged feebly before the emotionless, plastic mask. The curved blade of the butcher's knife clanked against the metal door as the fiend lowered the length of the weapon like a paper cutter toward her throat...

BABYSITTER MASSACRE: DADDY'S LITTLE KILLER

David O'Hanlon

New Dynamic Books

Firstly, this book wouldn't have been possible
without the following people—
Ashten Surgener, Henrique Couto, Vic Sage, Chris
Bearden, Julia Reed, Kait Holloway, Elizabeth
Fonken, Dan Wilder, Dahlia DeWinters, Mya Lairis,
Alex Loch, and Bill Mattison.

So, blame them if you hate it…

Secondly, there are so many people that deserve
their own dedication page, that I hate to do one at
all. I can never create a comprehensive enough list
of all the people that have made my path possible
through the years of support, love, dedication, and
inspiration. I've said, and will continue to say, that a
writer should never write for themselves—we write
for our fans. Thank you all for everything you've
done for me. But specifically—

To Brad Carter,
For teaching an uneducated reprobate how to put
his imagination to use. Everything I know I learned
from, or because of, you. I couldn't have gotten
this far without you suffering through so many
horrid manuscripts and half-cocked ideas. Everyone
reading this book owes you a debt of gratitude.

That's it for now.
I hope you'll all join me for the next nightmare,

-David O'Hanlon

FOREWORD

Before we go head-first into the bloody and sleazy escapism contained within this fright story I just wanted to take a moment to say thank you. When I created Babysitter Massacre in 2012 I had no idea how much it would grow, how many people would connect with it or how much it would mean to me.

As this book is published we are waiting out the coronavirus pandemic so that we can finally bring the cinematic sequels to life. Until then, we are lucky enough to have a sick, twisted, and brilliant mind like David O'Hanlon to bring us a further taste of that universe.

A universe full of blood and guts, yet with a heavy dose of *Fear Street* books for good measure. It's as much in the vein of R.L. Stine as it is Jim Wynorski or Fred Olen Ray.

So for you lovers of slashers and silly teen horrors, this one is for you. Get cozy so this book can make you squirm!

Henrique Couto
Creator of *Babysitter Massacre* film franchise (and now books!)

CONTENTS

PROLOGUE

October 29th, 1996

Aileen Sauer loved autumn in the Arkansas River Valley. She took off work early to stop in at Hallows Evil Costume Emporium—one of those pop-up Halloween stores that occupied the carcass of the ShowBiz Pizza Place for two brief months each year. Aileen was excited to get home and surprise the family with the matching costumes she'd found. They'd be the Three Little Pigs with their cute, but creepy, masks and gore-spattered coveralls. She even got the matching Big Bad Wolf for the hubby.

The isolate road from Kohler wound through the verdant sea of spinach on either side awaiting its final harvest of the year. Ahead of her, the foothills of the Boston Mountains were a wash of orange, red, and yellow leaves set ablaze by the sinking sun. She wanted to get home before Howard and make Halloween cookies to accompany the grand reveal of the costumes. Copper Creek was high from the previous day's nonstop rain and the surface sparkled as it rolled gently to join the river two miles south. Aileen smiled at the sight of the old truss bridge ahead and eased the accelerator down a little more, knowing she was almost to her final destination.

The little Ford Aspire bounced over the hump where the bridge met the road and zipped around the bend. Aileen slowed enough to wave at the Reid boys playing catch in their yard before turning onto the private road that twisted back to her house. The sun was reduced to spears of light stabbing through the canopy of weeping branches that merged over the narrow, one-lane path. She rolled her eyes as the house came into view.

Stacy Borman's LeBaron was sitting in the driveway, blocking the half of the garage Aileen used. She'd asked the babysitter to park along the side of the house where she wouldn't be in the way of whichever Sauer got home first.

Aileen shook her head. She would just have to move her car later. She wasn't about to let a minor inconvenience ruin her excitement. She pulled beside the house and slipped the car into park. She grabbed the ghoulishly branded bags from Hallows Evil and skipped across the walkway to the front door.

Aileen could hear the Spice Girls coming from the radio as she turned the key and stepped inside. Aileen blamed the eighties for ruining music. The British bimbos exemplified all the excess the previous decade idolized and she could hardly turn on the radio without hearing that damn song. At least it would fade out, like those sorts of songs always did. She still had plenty of real music on cassette for the long, daily commute. She hung the bags on the coat hooks and slipped her shoes off to store on the rack below.

She never noticed the disgusting moaning in the background of the song before and shuddered slightly. She'd ask Stacy to wear headphones if she was going to listen to that one. As she walked into the living room, the moans became more pronounced however. Then she heard words between them—words that included her husband's name.

The slapping of skin gained speed and broke with the rhythm of the song. Aileen inched into the room, chewing her lip anxiously. A foot adorned in the knee-high socks of a Kohler High uniform stuck up in the air over the back of the couch. The stockinged toes curled with another profane exclamation. Aileen's fists squeezed tightly until her festive, orange nails drew blood from her palms.

Stacy's blonde hair flipped over the arm of the couch with an ecstatic squeal. Aileen moved around the other side of the couch. Howard's pale, chubby ass pumped away at the teen while he grunted like a rutting hog. Aileen watched with her hurt rapidly turning to fury. He would have been finished and snoring already if it were Aileen beneath him. The little slut was apparently worth more effort than his wife.

"Fucking pound it," Stacy groaned between clenched teeth.

Howard's thrusts became more frantic. He didn't even put his dirty dishes in the sink like Aileen asked. He just piled them up to the side with shit still clinging to them... but he obeyed the putrid commands of the teen whore like a loyal dog. Aileen saw the Father-of-the-Year trophy she got him for Father's Day and snatched it off the fireplace mantle.

"Oh God," Stacy cried. "I'm coming"

"Yes, you are!" Aileen swung the trophy down.

Stacy's blue eyes opened just in time to see the granite base streaking toward her. The bridge of her nose shattered and the second shot split her forehead. Aileen screeched and hammered with the trophy. Blood splattered Howard's face and he rolled off the babysitter, spewing obscenities.

His wife's face contorted into a hellish grin while her shrieks turned to cackling laughter. The girl's dislodged eye bobbed on its nerve like a yoyo as her face collapsed from the blows. Still, Aileen swung again and again until she struck brain matter. She stood over the teen, heaving with deep breaths, and turned slowly to face Howard.

Her husband struggled to his feet, leaving his pants around his ankles and his deflated cock shrinking back like frightened turtle. He held his hands up and patted the air, taking a tentative step forward.

"Now, honey, let's just talk about this," he stammered.

"Talk?" Aileen tucked a strand of hair behind her ear, dislodging a piece of Stacy's skull from the auburn shock. "What's there to talk about, dear?"

"It's… well… it's not my fault." Howard nodded, convinced of his strategy. "She was sleeping on the job. And, you see, I got home early. Yeah, it was slow today, so I left early. I wanted to surprise you."

"Oh, you did." She licked at the spatter dripping across her lips. "You did that very well."

"I wasn't trying to do anything wrong." Howard shuffled closer to her. "Stacy was sleeping and I tried to wake her up. I wanted to tell her that wasn't acceptable. You know, because she's the sitter. What if something happened, right?"

"What if?" Aileen let the trophy hang at her side.

"Exactly!" Howard smiled unsteadily. His eyes flicked to the side—to a creeping shadow in the hall—then back to his deranged wife. "I just wanted to wake her up. But the way she was laying there, it just wasn't right. It's not the way you sleep, you know. It's like she was asking me to do something and when I woke her up, she was. She was just lying there, begging for it."

Aileen's knuckles popped as her fingers tightened around the gold-plated figure in his Superman pose. "Was she?"

"I'm sorry," Howard changed direction with his argument. "I should've showed more restraint... yeah, I definitely should have done that." His eyes lit up. A better lie came to him. "She was going to say I tried something."

"You did more than try, lover," Aileen said. The words oozed like a widow's venom. "You did a lot more."

"Right, I know." He took another step, putting himself between Aileen and the coffee table. "But she would have said something worse if I didn't give her what she wanted. I did what I thought was best for everyone. You don't think I wanted to do it, do you?"

Aileen swung the makeshift club and Howard lunged backwards, tripping over his slacks and falling through the glass table top. His legs draped over the tubular frame with his broad shoulders bending the opposite end flat. He groaned and rubbed his head, finding it slick from the smack against the hardwood floor. Distracted by the crimson wetness rolling down his fingertips, he didn't see Aileen kneel beside him. His wife stroked his cheek lovingly. He cried out at the touch as if her fingers were hot pokers. Aileen made shushing sounds before gripping his jaw between her nails.

"Oh, Howie," she whispered with her other hand moving through the debris. "The way you're lying there, dear, it's like you're begging me... just begging me... to stick it in."

The broken glass slipped under his jaw, severing the artery. Howard's life sprayed across the shards of the tabletop turning the floor into a gory mosaic of murder. Aileen twisted the weapon, opening the wound wider. Sobs broke up her maniacal laughter in an uneven tempo with more stabs. She turned her face away from Howard's vacant gaze and found herself staring at him still... through the cracked pane of the family portrait that previously occupied the coffee table. There they all were smiling up at her as one happy familial unit—the Sauer Patch, Howie always called them.

Aileen's fingers tightened on the shard. She looked at the demolished face of Stacy hanging over the arm of the couch. The babysitter's hair was stained pink. A slimy piece of gray matter slid down the strands and plopped onto the floor. Her school blouse was open and Aileen scowled. Three pounds of fat wrapped in perky, teenage flesh outweighed nine years of marriage.

"This is all your fault," Aileen whimpered. "You ruined everything. You murdered Howie, you whore."

Aileen brought her hand up, sticking the point of the glass into her own neck and dragging it across her throat. She felt the hand on her shoulder a moment too late. The slim fingers curled into her soft flesh and she turned to see the Street Sharks pajamas beyond the outstretched arm and Ryan's dark eyes staring into hers. Her lips trembled under the weight of the apology she croaked out.

"Mommy," Ryan said. "You're bleeding."

Aileen collapsed across Howard's corpse. Her mouth opened and closed, trying to catch an evasive breath. Ryan leaned over her and picked up the family portrait from the crimson pool. Aileen's vision blurred. She watched Ryan's bare feet pad across the living room to Stacy's dead body. The child flipped the quilt off the back of the couch over the babysitter and turned to face Aileen, slumped over Howard. Ryan hugged the portrait tightly.

"I love you, mommy," Ryan whispered before disappearing back into the hallway.

Aileen cried silently over Howard's remains. She wanted to tell Ryan "I love you too. Mommy always loves you," but she couldn't make words with her ravaged throat. She couldn't do much of anything, in fact, as she bled out in the ruins of the coffee table. As the world got darker, Aileen's mind wandered to the strangest thought amidst the chaos.

Why wasn't Ryan crying?

CHAPTER ONE

October 29, 2020

Larkin Combs took a deep breath and rang the video doorbell. It was Lark's first job with the Kohler Babysitter's Club. The club had been her idea, but she never really planned on being a part of it. Mercedes, Piper, and Linda were the popular, outgoing ones. Despite her bright smile, sweet nature, and fun-loving personality, Larkin was not one for socializing. She tried it, but it was always awkward and dialed her anxiety straight to eleven.

Then Larkin found out about the *au pair* program in nearby Fort Smith.

As soon as she finished with her Associate's Degree, she'd have all the requirements to attend Trinity College in Dublin. The *au pair* program would place her with a family in Ireland. Then she'd have a place to stay and money for school in exchange for taking care of the host family's kiddos. It was everything she dreamed of since she was a little girl. However, she still needed a year of professional childcare experience to qualify for the program. The babysitter's club would provide that, plus additional references and pad her bank account for life abroad.

Lark's face stretched into a wide, beaming smile in excitement. She was exactly one year away from getting on a plane and living her dreams. Few people could say they were going to do that. Fewer still had a plan to accomplish it. Almost none however, actually knew the date those dreams would become reality. Lark tried not to squeal with the building giddiness boiling within.

Her future started right here, on the doorstep of Britt and Erin Mercer.

"Just a moment," a voice called out as melodically as the tinkling windchimes hanging over the covered porch.

Lark straightened her shirt and reached for her ponytail, trying to decide if she should let her hair down or leave it back. She paused, gripped the scrunchie, let go, tugged again, dropped her hands. Her stomach twisted with anxiety. She felt foolish having a crisis over how to wear her hair. A blurry form filled the beveled window of the front door. Her time was up and the decision was made for her. She sighed and tried to put her smile back on as the lock clicked out of place and the knob turned.

Don't be weird. Don't say anything stupid. Don't laugh like a stoned hyena, she reminded herself. *Ten minutes of adulting and they'll be out of the house. Kids are easy. You've been practicing for this all afternoon.*

Erin Mercer did not look like a mother of two. Auburn curls splayed over her shoulders, left bare by the strapless navy dress that hugged her hourglass form. A gold chain belt with heart-shaped links circled her narrow waist and rested atop her hips. A matching necklace with three interlocking hearts hung over her ample breasts. Her face was tastefully made up with smoky eyeshadow that brought out the specks of gold in her green eyes and her lipstick was the color of a deep bruise that worked harmoniously with the dress. She looked like a movie star headed for the red-carpet premier of her new film.

Larkin tried not to think about her own appearance.

She failed.

Her Arkansas Razorbacks baseball shirt and maroon bellbottoms had seemed so cute when she finally decided on them after a forty-minute self-debate in front of her closet mirror. Her Converse sneakers twisted nervously into the boards beneath them. Her dishwater hair in its simple ponytail probably made her look lazy. And the last time she'd put on makeup, it took her three hours and she looked like clown college reject turned prostitute.

Fuck, I'm such a loser.

"You must be Lark," Erin said with a smile too bright and too wide to be ingenious and extended her hand. "Linda told us you were always prompt."

That's it? That's all she told you? Lark tried to keep smiling and gingerly shook with Missus Mercer.

"I am," Lark said. "Both, I mean. I am Lark and I am prompt." A nervous giggle made it through before she could stop it.

Erin laughed. "Linda said you were adorable too."

Like a retarded puppy. Lark fought the urge to sprint to her car and cry in the driveway.

"That's a good sign," Erin continued. "She's two-for-two already, so I'm sure that means she was telling the truth about your other qualities."

"I sure you'll be very satisfied, ma'am." Lark nodded softly. "I love working with kids."

"Come inside and I'll introduce you to them." Erin stepped aside and gestured for the teen to enter. "They're really great children, and very self-reliant, just far too young to be home alone."

Erin shut the door and led the way into the living room. It looked like something out of a magazine. A massive entertainment center occupied a space between dual bay windows where houseplants hung with their leafy tendrils dangling over padded benches. Immediately to Lark's left was a short wall that adjoined that one with built-in shelving for a vast movie collection. An oversized sofa sat in front of the TV with end tables at each arm and continuing to the right was a sight that drew an audible gasp of appreciation from Lark.

Three plushily carpeted, white steps led into the round conversation pit with its integrated seating wrapping around in a grand, red circle. A coffee table occupied the center with a laminated top over a collage of family photos. Erin led her past the space with a sweep of her hand. She was rattling off the amenities of the entertainment suite, but Lark was too busy taking in visual overload of the home.

Paintings lined the walls, mostly abstracts with vivid splashes of color exploding across the canvas in a guided chaos that made Lark's eyes work to find the images hidden within. All of them were done in black and red with purple highlights to contrast the hidden subject of each.

Erin caught the girl lingering over one.

"It's a wolf," she said with a satisfied smile. "I painted the entire series."

"They're amazing," Lark said. "Do you sell your paintings?"

Erin laughed. "Oh yes. That's what I do in fact. I take it Linda didn't tell you much about us, then?"

Lark shook her head.

"That's quite alright. Britt owns Copper Creek Estates, the housing firm. He designed their entire catalog himself, as well as our own home. We use my art in the display units and buyers often commission pieces from there. We have a studio out in the country where I can work and Britt can make his models for new homes."

"That sounds awesome. It must be nice having your own retreat to get away and focus on your art."

"Oh, it really is. I try to spend a week out there every few months just to build my catalog. I sell quite a bit out of the Bastion Gallery in Fort Smith and do a yearly showing at the Le Fleur in New York." Erin's face glowed with pride over the couple's achievements. She guided Lark into the kitchen.

Lark took mental notes as Erin ran down the contents of the cabinets and fridge. She opened a door set to the side of the stove to reveal a cavernous pantry with a deep freeze resting in the back. Lark grew up with a single mom, living paycheck to paycheck and had never seen so many groceries stockpiled at one time. Her stomach growled at the possibilities as Erin welcomed her to try whatever she was in the mood for.

The tour continued back into the living room and up the stairs that were wide enough for the two women to walk side-by-side. A playroom waited at the top of the steps where eight-year-old Branch played on a tablet in the cozy embrace of a beanbag chair. He looked up from the screen long enough to wave. Erin shook her head.

"That's about as social as Branch gets," she said. "Branch Lincoln Mercer, come over here and introduce yourself to your new babysitter."

"What's wrong with the one I have?" the boy whined while fiercely tapping the screen. "Linda is fun and helps me find strategies for my games."

"Linda is sick, honey. Maybe you and Lark can make her a get well soon card," Erin said.

"Yeah, I bet that would help her recover extra quick," Lark lied.

Linda wasn't sick at all and Lark knew it. The Mercers were Linda's most profitable customers. They went out for date night every Thursday and paid twice the normal rate. They also tipped generously if there were any hiccups such as upset tummies, homework assistance, or delayed returns. She wasn't about to lose the contract for a date.

However, that date was with none other than Steve Fitzhugh, heir apparent to the Fitzhugh spinach dynasty. Steve was a bad boy by choice with a million-dollar trust fund and a pro wrestler's body. Linda spent the last two years of high school trying to get a date with Kohler's most eligible delinquent and wasn't about to miss her shot. And so, Lark, always there for a friend, got the call to fill in while Linda got filled in.

"Did she happen to mention what was wrong with her, dear?" Missus Mercer asked.

"Oh, yeah." Lark nodded. "She's got a stomach bug. She ate at one of those sketchy food trucks downtown yesterday."

"Horrible things. I doubt any of them even have permits." Erin put her hands on her hips and whistled. "Branch, I said come here."

The boy huffed and tapped the screen a couple more times before skulking to the door and extending his hand. "My name's Branch. It's a pleasure to meet you."

"It's a pleasure to meet you, too." Lark shook Branch's hand before leaning in conspiratorially. She looked over her shoulder at Erin for effect, then back to Branch. "And I know where to find the best strategies for games. I taught Linda, in fact."

"Swell," he said unconvincingly.

Lark gave him a wink and tousled his hair before continuing with Erin down the hall. Missus Mercer pointed out the spare room, Branch's room, the guest bathroom, the linen closet, the laundry room, and the door that led to the attic— which was always to remain locked. Erin was suspiciously adamant about that. Lark's amazement over the Mercers' lack of practicality and thrift was disrupted by the click of a door and a rolling wall of steam.

Britt Mercer emerged from the manmade fogbank roughly towel-drying his black hair. He stopped suddenly and smiled with delight at his wife. He kissed her cheek.

"There you are, my love. I decided to use the guest bathroom in case you needed to apply a second coat." Britt glanced at Lark and his smile turned to a hungry, razor slash of white teeth between thin lips. "And you must be the new Linda.

I don't think I've seen a sequel surpass the original quite so well."

Lark put her hands behind her and tapped her fingers against the opposite palm to calm the stirring anxiety. She realized she was holding her breath but was too nervous to let it out. Mister Mercer's body apparently stopped aging in college. Lark tried to look away from his predatory smile only to find herself following the beads of water rolling across his sinuous chest. The droplets continued down his torso and over a tattoo of a winking, cartoon pig protruding from the towel around his waist. Britt put the hair towel over his neck and pulled at it, giving his muscles a flex for Lark's benefit. She knew full well it wasn't a coincidence that he stepped out of the shower half-naked at exactly that time.

And judging by the look on her face, Erin knew it as well.

"I better finish getting ready." Britt put on his loving husband mask as he turned to his wife. "I know how much you despise tardiness."

"Amongst other things. Do hurry." Erin watched her husband stalk away and disappear into the master bedroom before she addressed Lark again. Her hostess-grade smile had returned. "Forgive my husband, please. He spent too many years in a fraternity and I fear keg stands and bong rips might have left him with permanent brain damage. Let me introduce you to our other son."

They walked past the door of the master

bedroom, which Britt had left cracked. He stood at the end of the bed, just visible through the narrow gash. Lark glanced at the door innocently... and Britt let the towel drop. Larkin turned her head back quickly and Erin knocked on the door of her youngest child.

"Stone is a quiet boy," Erin turned her head as she said it, spotting Britt over Lark's shoulder. She cleared her throat. "He's only six, but is so much cleverer than the other children his age. He loves being helpful too."

The door squeaked open and a diminutive child with eyes too big for his button nose stared up at Lark. He smiled as best he could with three missing teeth and waved happily.

"Hi. I'm Stone," he said giddily.

Lark felt her muscles unwind and her stomach settle at the sight of the tiny child. Stone Mercer made her feel comfortable for the first time since she agreed to Linda's pleas. Little boys were so full of promise and love. Then somewhere along the way, they gestated into slimy, subhuman creatures like Britt Mercer and Hunter Hogan. Lark forced the festering memory of her ex to the back of her mind. That was a panic attack for another time.

Lark squatted down and straightened the collar of Stone's Scooby-Doo pajamas. "I'm Lark. It's really nice to meet you."

"Yep." Stone nodded. "I'm going to watch Scoob now."

And the door swung shut once again.

Yeah. This is going smooth.

Lark forced herself to smile before she stood back up and laughed softly. "I think we'll do just fine tonight, Missus Mercer."

CHAPTER TWO

Erin laced her arm around Britt's as they approached the ticket booth. The attendant wore a retro-styled Frankenstein mask with his Cine-Magic uniform. The monstrous plastic mask did nothing to disguise the disdain he held for his job.

"Welcome to CineMagic. Which fantastic film would you like to fall under the spell of to-night?" the teen said the repeated line drolly.

Erin smiled. "That's a great mask. You must love the classics. There's too much of," she waved at the other attendant in a slutty Jason Voorhees costume, "that stuff now. Horror used to mean something."

"Thanks." The kid's voice perked up. It was really just the only thing he could afford on his meager wage, but no one else was going to compliment him. Most of the customers weren't even getting in his line, in fact. He leaned closer to the speaker. "I'm not supposed to tell you because the manager is a cheapskate, but corporate told us anyone that says 'trick-or-treat' at the concession stand gets a free candy with a popcorn purchase."

"Thanks, kid. I'll take two tickets to *Shanks-*

giving 7: Just Desserts." Britt smirked. "I don't like my horror to mean shit."

The attendant nodded slowly and printed off the tickets. He slid them under the plexiglass partition. "Enjoy the massacre, sir."

"Oh, I always do." Britt collected the tickets and led his wife through the doors.

The lobby was the typical grandiose sprawl of gold-plated rails, velvet ropes, and soda-stained carpet adorned in the required splash of geometric patterns and movie theater clipart. Two ghosts, a vampire, and a dinosaur served the lines of moviegoers at the concession stand. Erin tugged Britt in the direction of the dinosaur. Date night was always the same. First, they went to Winchester's for the exact same meal that they ordered the week before. Then they went to see a movie and alternated who would pick it. Then they stopped by the Wise Penny for a drink while they discussed the film before heading home. The Mercers liked routine.

As such, Erin was simultaneously biting her bottom lip and twirling her hair in the way she did whenever she was nervous. Linda had been their date night sitter for the last two years. She blew a hard breath between her lips and turned to Britt.

"I don't like the new sitter," she grumped.

Britt rolled his eyes. "What's wrong with her?"

"Nothing, I suppose." Erin waited to say anything else. "We know Linda. She follows the rules and takes care of the boys. Lark is a variable, that's all. I'm sure she'll do just fine, but I would have preferred we postpone and use Linda, like always. We know we can trust her by now."

"Is that so?" Britt nudged Erin's side and tilted his head toward the vampire's line. "Pay attention to your surroundings, my love. Carelessness is costly."

"That little cunt." Erin's lips tightened.

Linda twisted her mahogany curls around her fingers while her date prattled on about something that she clearly only feigned interest in. His hand slithered down the small of her back and he leaned down to kiss her. Linda's short stature made the man work for it. They made out in the lobby until another patron told them to keep the line moving. The statuesque date glared at the interloper over his bulging shoulder and grabbed a handful of Linda's curvaceous attributes before stepping forward and addressing the counter clerk.

Erin fixed her stare back on Britt. "She lied to us."

"I suppose that could be her doctor with his hand on her ass," Britt said with a chuckle. "Though I believe his practice is in gynecology."

"We should say something." Erin took a step out of line when Britt pulled her back and wrapped an arm around her waist.

"What did I just say about carelessness?" Britt guided her forward as the line moved. "We're going to get you some Sour Patch Kids like you like and we're going to go see our movie like we planned. Date nights are for us, my love. We can get more of anything, except for time. Don't let a foolish little girl steal it from us."

"Aren't you upset about this?"

"Undoubtedly." He shrugged. "I'm going to devour two boxes of Whoppers over the whole traumatic experience. There goes my weekly carb intake."

Erin watched the young lovebirds order their drinks and snacks. Linda was clearly upset by whatever her date had said and slapped his hand away before grabbing the popcorn from the counter and storming down the corridor to the auditorium their movie was playing in. Erin smiled again. At least Linda's night wasn't going according to plan.

Once they got their candy, popcorn, and diet sodas, the Mercers proceeded down the opposite hallway to find their own screening room. Erin cursed under her breath as she entered the darkened chamber beyond the red LED sign displaying the movie's title. She despised slasher flicks and the *Shanksgiving* series was the bottom of the slimy barrel. Britt made her watch every single of them back-to-back each November.

Erin glanced at her husband and saw the childlike excitement in his eyes. If there was a masked killer, Britt thought it was art. And this was the first *Shanksgiving* sequel in fifteen years, so he was even more thrilled. She'd suffer through it and make him order the Chave Hermitage for her nightcap at Wise Penny's in retaliation. At $85 a glass, it might make Britt rethink his cinematic tastes.

They took their seats in the back of the nearly-empty auditorium. The Thanksgiving-themed franchise had been losing steam since '98, but somehow still pulled in enough to garner this final theatrical release. Britt leaned back in the seat and rested his head on the wall as the previews played on the big screen. He groaned. Britt hated film trailers—they gave away too much of the film. He pressed a button on his watch to check the time.

"Maybe this is the last one before the show," he whispered.

"Yeah."

"You're still thinking about Linda, huh?"

"Of course." Erin twisted in her seat. "She lied. You know how I feel about dishonesty."

"Yes, my love. That's why I said we'll deal with it in the morning." He took his phone from his pocket and flipped it to silent. "I'll check on the kids really quick. Let's just enjoy the movie."

She sniffed and shook her head with a giggle. "You know I'm not going to enjoy *this* movie."

"Well," Britt paused to finish texting Larkin. His thumbs tapped the letters and looked up at his wife. "You're still as beautiful as you were in college."

"Is that so?"

"Remember how we used to see these movies back then?" He pressed send and tucked the phone away before reaching over and gripping Erin by the back of the neck. He pulled her close and kissed her.

She nipped his lip. Britt recoiled. Erin watched the screen's light illuminate a drop of blood forming and kissed it away. Her nails dug into his thigh and she slipped her tongue into his mouth. He sucked at the invading muscle and squeezed her neck tighter. Erin's hand moved higher and he stiffened against her palm. She leaned away, rubbing him through his slacks.

"I don't remember ever getting to see the movie from where I was sitting," she whispered and worked his zipper. "I don't mind missing another one."

Britt lifted his hips to help her free his erection. He pressed her head down and moaned a long, slow "fuck" as her mouth slipped over him. His fingers twisted in her hair while her pink lips glided methodically down his shaft. The phone buzzed in his jacket pocket and he checked the babysitter's reply. Erin's teeth scrapped him gently on the trip back up and she worked her tongue teasingly before taking him down her throat again.

"I think…" Britt groaned and tried to speak again, "I think we should just get rid of Linda."

Erin purred an agreement without breaking

her rhythm.

"Yeah, I thought you'd like that." Britt rocked his hips to match her movements. "I think Lark will be just great." He closed his eyes as she quickened her pace. "Ouch!"

Erin pulled her head away with a wet pop. She shrugged. "Sorry, I got carried away."

"It happens." Britt thumbed open the box of Whoppers and nodded for his wife to continue. He tipped the malt balls into his mouth and smiled around them as the feature presentation began. "Just in time."

CHAPTER
THREE

Larkin pulled the blankets snug under Stone's chin and poked his nose like a button. She lifted the stuffed animal from beside his pillow. The bear had oversized buttons for eyes and dreadlocks sticking out of a colorful rasta cap.

"This is a strange toy," she mused.

"Dad won him at the fair." Stone pouted suddenly. "I didn't win anything. I'm not strong enough. Couldn't throw the ball far enough. Couldn't swing the hammer hard enough. Nothing."

"Have you ever been to the river?" Lark asked sweetly.

The boy nodded.

"Rivers are strong. They can push a whole car away and pull trees out of the ground." She slipped the Rastafarian bear under the edge of the comforter beside the child. "Then one day that big, mighty river comes crashing into a boulder —a stone, just like you—and that stone doesn't move. It stands its ground and the whole river has to change direction or stop in its tracks."

"One stone can do that?"

"That's right." She smiled and stroked his hair. "There's different ways to be strong. The river is noisy so it can tell everyone how much strength it has, but the stone is silent and changes the world simply by refusing to get out of the way."

"You're much smarter than Linda." Stone sat up and hugged her. "Will you come watch me again?"

"I hope so," she said sincerely. "But right now, you're all untucked again."

They both giggled and Larkin fixed his blankets. She clicked on the Scooby-Doo lamp and left the room with a final goodnight before shutting off the overhead light and heading to Branch's room. The Mercer's eldest was absent and, not surprisingly, still in the playroom tapping wildly at the iPad.

"Crap!" he threw his head back against the beanbag with a sigh. "Every stinking time."

Larkin rapped the doorframe. "Tough level?"

"Huh?" Branch looked up and shook his head. "Oh, no. It's multiplayer. I lagged at the worst time." He sighed dramatically and threw his hands in the air. "Again."

"It's probably for the best. For starters, I need to get you to bed." She held her hand out for the tablet. "Come on, I'll plug it in so it's ready for you in the morning."

Branch hesitated and then let a soft grin ease onto his face. "Okay, I'll go to bed, but how could losing be for the best?"

Lark tucked the iPad under her arm and put the other around his shoulders as they walked to his room. "Losing shows us where we can improve."

"I guess." Branch pushed open the door.

The room was structurally the same as Stone's, but decorated in video game posters and the boy's own artwork. Larkin spotted the bank of assorted chargers on his desk and set the tablet there, plugging it in and going to the bed to turn back the sheets.

Branch sat on the edge and laid back, letting the sitter pull the blankets over him. "Do you play games?"

"On occasion." She scanned the room quickly and found a poster she recognized. "I like *Hello Neighbor*."

"That's so first grade," he snorted. "I'm playing a horror game called *The Thing Within*. One player is the monster from outer space that crashes at a summer camp and the rest are campers. The monster has to eat all the campers."

"Who plays the monster?" Lark had seen the gameplay videos her cousin watched and already knew, but she loved listening to children's excitement when they got to explain their activities. "Is it scary?"

"The monster is randomly picked. As a camper, it's super scary." The boy turned on his side and folded his pillow in half. "But playing as the monster is the hardest."

"Why's that?"

"There's lots of ways for the campers to win. You can kill the monster, of course. But that's what all the noobs try to do. You can capture the monster too, which is nearly impossible. Most players try to turn on the spaceship's reactor and blow you up, but they have to find all the pieces to put it back together first."

"Sounds like playing the monster *is* super difficult." The sitter nodded sagely. "So, the more campers that are uneaten, the faster they can meet the win conditions?"

"Exactly!" Branch's face exploded into a smile. "It always lags when I use my teleport power. You can only use it once each round, so I save it until the end because the players split up to keep the monster from winning. Linda was supposed to help me figure it out tonight, but I guess she got sick."

"Hmm." Lark pulled her knees to her chest and ran through what she remembered her cousin telling her about the game. "What if you used the teleport when there were more players in the game. Then the lag wouldn't be an issue."

"That's a good point." Branch scratched at his curls. "But when would I use it?"

Lark rubbed his shoulder and pretended to think about it. "Well, a reactor sounds like a pretty secure place, like there'd only be one way in."

"Well, yeah." Branch sat up on his elbow. "It's at the end of this long hall."

"So, if they need to go back to the reactor, you could go there first. They'll think they have you trapped and then you can use the doorway like a funnel to eat them one at a time."

"But if they get through and I teleport to safety, they'll just start the reactor."

Lark held up a finger in an ah-ha reveal. "That's why you teleport into the hallway and trap them. Call it Camper Barrel, because it's going to be all you can eat."

"Wow," Branch gasped. "You are way better at strategies than Linda."

"We'll keep that our little secret," Larkin held a finger to her lips and winked.

"Nothing wrong with being second best." Branch snuggled his head into the pillow. "It can teach her how to improve, after all."

"That's true. Goodnight, sweetie."

Larkin left Branch's room when her phone chimed. She took it from her pocket and checked the message.

Have you checked on the kids? it read.

She responded that she did and continued downstairs to the movie shelf. Her phone chimed again. She traced her finger along the spines of the meticulously organized collection. She didn't expect so many campy horror films in the Mercer collection and she giggled at some of the titles. Her finger stopped on one called *Dollman vs Demonic Toys* and she decided that was a must-see title. Lark checked her phone and felt her pulse race.

You're going to talk to me, it said.

The number was new, but it always was.

No, I'm not, she thought. There was no point texting back.

Hunter was using a text app to message her. Until he committed a real crime, the cops wouldn't check his internet history to prove it was him sending the messages. Lark doubted anything short of her murder would be enough to gain their interest. If that did the trick, even.

She had blocked his phone number and all his social media accounts. He simply created new accounts until she finally shut down hers as well. Larkin's number had been changed three times in the four months since she broke up with Hunter. Each time, he somehow learned the new one.

The opposite side of the street was public property that sat ten feet past the limits of her protection order, so he could park there and watch her house at night. He would leave notes nailed to the tree there for her. People like Hunter Ray Hogan never left the town they were born in. She was stuck with him until she moved away, or he found someone else to terrorize. Larkin deleted the message without responding.

In the kitchen, she found the mixing bowls and set the largest of them on the counter before going into the pantry for the primary requirement of any babysitter's diet… the popcorn. She tossed the bag into the microwave and jabbed the popcorn button. Lark set up her movie as the kernels began exploding in the background like buttery gunfire. She remembered Erin mentioning something about the inputs during the tour, but she had been too awestruck to pay attention. After several tries, she got the DVD menu on the screen. Her phone rang and she stared at the display.

Unknown number.

She answered the call against her better judgment.

"It's about time," Hunter's voice said.

"Stop bothering me. You're not allowed to call me," she reminded him.

"Prove that I did." He tsked three times. "You don't want to run around making false accusations. You might hurt my feelings. You remember what happens when you hurt my feelings, don't you my little bird?"

"Fuck you, Hunter." Larkin pressed the end call icon and stuck the phone in her pocket.

The popcorn wasn't popping anymore, despite the whirring of the still-running microwave. Larkin sighed and cursed. She went to the microwave and opened the door, crinkling her nose at the wafting odor.

"Why do they even put the stupid popcorn button on the microwave, if it's just going to burn the popcorn?" She held the bag at arm's length and proceeded out the back door so she didn't stink the place up any more than she already had.

Lark stepped off the porch and rounded the back of the house to find the big, green trash-cans sitting next to the gate. She gave the can her burnt offering and let the lid bang shut, startling a stray out of the shadows. Lark screamed before she could clamp her hands over her mouth. The scrawny, orange-white tom sprang up and over the fence.

"Stupid cat!" she hissed. "Yeah, you better run."

She leaned against the siding and laughed softly. Her heart eased into a more rhythmic thumping after a moment. The cat meowed on the other side of the fence.

Probably telling its friends how it scared the stupid human.

Around the corner, she heard the door slam shut. She shrieked again and slap a palm against the house.

"Damn it, Larkin! Get ahold of yourself," she huffed. "There's nothing to be afraid of. Not any-more."

She came around the house and jogged up the steps of the back porch. The door had blown shut.

Of course that's what happened, she soothed herself.

Larkin shut the door behind her and locked it, then went to check on the boys. Branch was snoring loudly and drooling on his *Five Nights at Freddy's* pillowcase. Lark backed out of his room and found Stone in much the same condition, only he'd kicked off his blankets. She snuck in and replaced the covers over him before going downstairs to watch the movie, sans popcorn.

Lark made it to the bottom of the stairs and froze in place, shaking her head and swallowing hard.

Hunter sat on the far side of the conversation pit, patting the red upholstery for her to join him.

CHAPTER FOUR

Linda crossed her arms and twisted in the truck seat away from Steve as he leaned in to kiss her. He banged his forehead against the steering wheel.

"Why are you acting like this?" he groaned.

"I knew you were stupid rich, but now I see you're just plain stupid." Linda turned to face him. "You're a penny-pinching, tightwad."

"You stay rich by not blowing money on dumb shit." Steve shrugged. "We grow spinach, not pot. We have to be frugal."

"Frugal is using a coupon." Linda used her arms to push up her tits closer to the plunging neckline. "Cheap is missing out on the hottest body in Kohler because you didn't want to buy Milk Duds."

"You can't be serious?"

Linda opened the door and stepped out. "Hope you weren't too frugal to buy a Fleshlight because you're not getting into my bed!"

She slammed the door for emphasis and stormed to her apartment. Her plump ass wiggled seductively with each determined step. She looked back over her shoulder when she got to the front door and saw Steve still watching. Linda let the keys fall and bent over seductively to pick them up. She unlocked the deadbolt and stepped inside, turning to blow Steve a kiss off her middle finger.

The F150's tires squealed as it left the curb and Linda shut the door. She took her phone out of her jacket pocket and flipped on the camera app on her way to the bathroom. Linda pushed her lips out like a duck and snapped the first selfie before turning on the shower. She adjusted the water carefully, tossed her shirt into the corner, and took another picture. The last pic made her grin smugly at the way the black lace fought to keep its prizes held inside. She laughed and sent both of them to Steve's phone.

"Your loss, cheapo." She sat the phone on the counter and headed back to her bedroom.

Linda kicked off her shoes, curling her toes in the carpet with a sigh. The evening had not gone according to plan, but she was sure, with a little teasing, Steve would come to the realization that she was worth the six-dollar Milk Duds. She undid the buttons on her jeans and moaned happily. The effort to get her impressive backside into the pants was paid back in the stares and catcalls they got her, but nothing was more rewarding than finally peeling them off.

Linda slipped the bra straps over her arms and flipped the cups down. She wiggled her freed breasts in front of the cheval mirror and debated sending another pic to Steve. She turned to examine her profile and turned a little toward the mirror.

"Oh girl! That's the shot right there."

She retrieved her phone and ignored Steve's three apologetic texts while she positioned herself again. She brought a finger to her mouth, nibbling the tip and strategically placing her picture-taking arm to cover her caramel nipples.

You're not sorry yet, but you will be, she typed. Once the text went through, she added the photo and sent, *Too cheap to buy sweets, too cheap to clap cheeks.*

She laughed at her cleverness when a text came through. It wasn't from Steve, but an unknown number.

How are you feeling?

"Shit. Mister Mercer must have gotten a new phone." She scowled at her own, cracked, screen. "Must be fucking nice to be rich."

A bit better. Gotta really sore throat, she replied.

The doorbell chimed with its chorus of electric church bells. Linda tossed her phone to the bed and pulled her hair up in a messy bun. Studying her reflection as the bell rang a second time, she grabbed her robe from the back of the door. Steve wasn't getting a free peek already. She would make him wait a couple days before she gave in. Linda pulled the robe on and went to the front door. She checked the peephole and saw no one on the other side.

"Don't give up too easy, Stevie Boy." She set the chain lock and eased the door open as far as it would go. "Hello?"

No one said anything.

"Quit fucking around, Steve." Linda pressed her face to the gap and looked in both directions for taillights. "I'm serious. Stop playing."

When the mysterious visitor refused to answer yet again, she shut and locked the door. On the way to the bathroom, Linda let the robe fall away and slipped out of her panties at the bathroom door. She discarded the thong into the corner with her shirt and bunched the cheetah-print shower curtain in her first. The phone chimed from the bedroom. She looked over her shoulder and grinned mischievously. Steve would just have to wait and maybe she'd feel charitable enough to tantalize him further.

She pulled the curtain aside and stepped in. Linda screamed, slipping in place and trying to get over the edge of the tub. She stood on the bathmat, dripping wet and shaking from the frigid blast.

"Fuck!" She reached for the knob and adjusted it again. "How's that shit even happen?"

Her wet feet slapped across the tile as she went back into the bedroom and let the shower heat again once again. Linda picked up the phone as saw more texts from Steve and another from

Mister Mercer.

Can't wait to see you, it said.

"Horny bastard. Can't just say 'get well soon' like a normal person?" Linda shrugged. "Then again, I wouldn't mind calling you daddy for a bit."

I can't wait, she typed back.

Steve wasn't the only rich guy with a rock-hard body, after all. And Britt Mercer had the edge in experience. Linda thought about both of them and chewed her lip before trotting back into the bathroom, giggling all the way.

"Thank God for massaging showerheads."

She pulled the curtain back and stepped in to find the water where she wanted it this time. Linda squeezed the bodywash onto her pouf. The sweet medley of berries tickled her nose while she worked up a lather across her torso and followed the fluffy, suds down her legs. The curtain tore away and Linda jumped. She slid and started to fall. The gloved hand caught her hair to hold her up.

"No! Stop it!" she cried, prying at the fingers out of her curls. "Somebody, help!"

Her attacker jerked her from the tub. Linda's face smacked against the porcelain back of the toilet. She pressed herself up, only for the callous, leather glove to clamp over her mouth from behind. The attacker twisted her head into position over the toilet bowl and waved the large chef's knife in front of her face. Linda tried to scream again.

The blade cut the vocal cords before they

could make a sound and pressed deeper into the tissue. Linda gurgled, choked, and bled neatly in the basin below her. She slumped down and rolled to the floor. The killer walked across her back, out of the bathroom. She fought to keep her eyes open. On the bed, her phone chimed with a new message. She crawled forward a few inches. Her killer was standing at the foot of her bed, looking at her phone. They stuffed it into the pocket of their black hoodie and left the room.

Linda gasped.

Coughed.

And died alone.

CHAPTER FIVE

Hunter Ray Hogan patted the seat next to him and pushed his hair off his narrow cheeks.

"I just want to talk to you," he said in his slow drawl.

He waved Larkin over and slapped the cushion, hard, three times. The babysitter shook her head and pointed to the door.

"This is ridiculous," she said. "You can't be this close to me and you definitely can't be here."

"You don't own this place. You can't throw me out." He licked his lips. "I always liked you in those pants. Way I see it, until the owner says something then I got as much right to be here as you."

"Bullshit." Larkin slipped her phone out of her back pocket. "I'm calling the cops."

"And telling them what?" Hunter stretched out and draped his arms across the floor behind him. "There's no sign of a break in and I'll be long gone by the time those fat pigs get here, so there won't be no sign of me neither."

Hunter laughed and slapped his thighs, jolting up and crossing the pit in a flash. He stepped up the opposite bench and got in front of Larkin.

"Go ahead and dial," he growled. His hands gripped Lark's arms and he massaged the tensing biceps with his thumbs. "They'll come running and get here to find nothing at all. I'll tell them I was with some other gal and they won't even ask who, they'll just say you found out and got all jealous. That's what they'll say. Or worse, they'll think you're nuttier than squirrel shit, just like your old man. Good luck getting them to come next time you call after that."

"Fuck you."

"After we talk, maybe." Hunter laughed. "See, I need you to understand where I'm coming from. You can't just put an end to something like we have."

"What you have is a fucking mental condition if you think we're talking about shit." Lark twisted her right arm away and shoved him back. "We dated for nine weeks, that was long enough. Hell, we've been broken up for almost twice that. Get a grip on yourself. I'm done with your sick ass."

Hunter's hand shot up and gripped Larkin by the back of the neck, pulling her face against his in a perverse mockery of affection. "Little bird, you won't never be done with me."

The front door opened and Erin Mercer came in, clearly irritated as she shut it and tossed her clutch to the small table opposite the coatrack. Her face twisted with curiosity as she entered the living room and saw the strange man with his hand on the babysitter's neck.

"I don't think I know you," she said sternly.

"That sure seems unfortunate on my part, ma'am." Hunter put on his best smile… the one he lured Larkin in with in the first place. "Lark was just telling me how gorgeous her new employer was, and I have to say she wasn't lying a bit."

"I'm pleased you think so," she replied facetiously. "Did Larkin let you in through the front door?"

"Why, yes ma'am she did. Anything else would've been improper," Hunter said, softly.

"Good, then you know where it is." Erin prowled past them. "Show yourself to it."

Hunter leaned his face next to Larkin's to feign a kiss. "We'll talk real soon."

"No." Lark locked eyes with him and dug her nails into her palm to keep from shaking. "You stay the hell away from me."

"You're going to come to your senses about all this," he said, squeezing her neck tighter before finally letting go and walking to the door. "Tell your boss I appreciate her having me over."

Once he was gone, Larkin ran to the door and locked it. She leaned her forehead against the glass and tried to compose herself before heading into the kitchen, guided by the clacking of Missus Mercer's heels on the tile. She watched the woman slap bread on the cutting board next to a package of lunch meat and individually wrapped cheese slices.

"Mister Mercer isn't with you," Lark pointed out.

Obviously. She fought the urge to correct herself.

"How astute." Erin opened the fridge and retrieved a jar of mayonnaise. She returned to the kitchen island. "Britt got called to the office. He'll catch an Uber back home when he's finished with his business. Why do you care?"

"I just meant," Larkin started.

You meant what, Lark? she asked herself. *She's already mad at you.*

"Britt works a lot. A good thing for you considering how you spent the evening," Erin said, pulling a chef's knife from the block.

"It wasn't what it looked like, Missus Mercer," Lark said softly. "I promise."

"Your occupation attracts a certain kind of girl." Erin jabbed the glistening steel into the jar for a glob of the condiment. "I learned that a long time ago. I was completely against hiring a sitter."

"I assure you, it won't happen again."

Tell her! Tell her the creep broke in and threatened you. Lark chewed the inside of her cheek, considering the option. *No, then she'll fire you for endangering her kids and never give you a recommendation. No job experience, no program. You'll be stuck in the dead-end, shit-kicking town forever.*

"It was a surprise," Lark lied. "I didn't even know he knew where I was. We're taking a break and he wanted to talk about it."

"Wanting to see other people? Sow your wild oats," Erin talked with her hands, flashing the knife like a symphony conductor. "Typical."

"Actually, I want to focus on the job and have more time to devote to the families I sit for." Larkin fought to hold back a curse. It wasn't the time to grow a backbone, but she was still fired up from the incident with Hunter. "I love children, Missus Mercer. It's important to me to be the best that I can be as a sitter. I'm going to school to be a teacher, in fact."

Erin finished piling her sandwich and cut it in half. "The kitchen stinks."

"Oh." Larkin looked at her shoes, watched the fabric flex as she wiggled her toes nervously inside. "I burned my popcorn earlier. I'm sorry."

"You can have the other half," Erin said as she pushed the offering across the cutting board with the blade. "Eat it on your way home."

Erin picked up her half and walked out of the kitchen. Larkin collected the other half, skulking through the living room to the front door.

"Oh, Larkin," Erin called from the top of the stairs.

Lark perked up. "Yes, ma'am?"

"Lock the door on your way out."

CHAPTER SIX

Larkin slapped the nightstand until she found her phone and shut off the alarm. She groaned and rolled out of bed. She did the trio of stretches she remembered from that week in junior high when she was crazy about yoga to get the kinks out. Sleep didn't come easy to her. It didn't leave easy either.

She pulled her nightshirt off and dropped it in the milk crate she used for a hamper. She planned on showering and going all out for her the meeting. Not only was it Friday, but it was the day before Halloween. The Kohler Babysitter's Club would be extra busy and wanted to take full advantage of the situation. Of course, Lark had optioned to take advantage of her snooze button instead. Larkin slid open the folding doors of her closet and groaned again.

"Fuck my life."

The two baskets of laundry she'd been meaning to put away were still there beneath the bar of mostly empty hangers. She grabbed her favorite peasant top—the one with the lace cutouts on the shoulders and the puffed sleeves that her friends called her "grandma blouse."

Screw them. It's cute, it's comfortable, and it goes with everything. She reached for the first pair of yoga pants she saw sticking out of a basket and wrestled them free. *Case and point.*

She went light on the makeup, doing just enough while her curling iron heated up to look like she made an effort. Once she finished, Lark pulled the plug by the cord, a habit that annoyed everyone in her life, and forced a smile at her reflection. She snatched the orange bottle from the shelf beside the mirror and took out two of the anxiety pills, swallowed them and tried the smile once more.

Lark finished her outfit with her fancy sandals and creaked down the stairs of the venerable townhouse. Her mother was asleep on the couch, still wearing the uniform from job number two. Lark smiled sadly and went to the kitchen to set the coffee pot up for her mom. The poor woman worked full-time at the hospital and still needed to pick up shifts at Hamburger Hamlet.

Of course, if you'd act like a grown-up and move out, she wouldn't need to, Larkin thought.

She set her mother's favorite mug next to the machine with two hazelnut creamer cups before going out to her car. She did a double-take at the object across the street. Notes from Hunter on cardboard signs were becoming so ordinary that she almost didn't notice. Larkin stormed across the street, fighting back tears.

The orange-and-white tomcat was pinned to the tree trunk with a hunting knife through its neck. The sign hung from the handle with its messaged scrawled in fat black lines of permanent marker:

BAD KITTY SCARED MY LITTLE BIRD

Larkin sank to her knees and sobbed.

Mercedes and Piper sat outside Beans and Things coffee shop awaiting Larkin's arrival. Mercedes sipped her Brookie frappe while absently clicking her acrylic nails on the metal table top. Piper blew a vape cloud into her face, making her cough... and stop clicking.

Piper laughed and leaned back in the chair, twirling a blonde lock around her fingers. "Do you think she knows?"

"No. If she knew, she would've called." Mercedes took another sip of her drink then looked to Piper suspiciously. "Wait. Why didn't you call her? You're the club president."

"I didn't save her number after she changed it *again* because of Florida-Georgia Psycho." Piper rolled her eyes and took a fruity drag off the vape pen. "I don't know what she saw in that loser. I mean, he lives in Hell's Bells for crying out loud."

The Silver Bells Motel, known locally as Hell's Bells, was a dozen single-room cabins. Beside it sat an empty field that had grown, over the last decade, into a sprawling, ad hoc trailer park full of collapsing single-wides, RVs, vans, and even one shipping container. The chaotic jumble became home for the ex-cons, sex offenders, meth cooks and other undesirables that the residents wanted to keep out of Kohler. The place was located a half-mile south of the railroad overpass that marked the end of Kohler's city limits... and the responsibilities of the local police.

Anything goes, in Hell's Bells.

"I don't think she knew that at the time." Mercedes twisted the straw, making it squeak against the plastic lid. "Wasn't it your party they met at?"

Piper glared at her, but her reply was cut off by Larkin's arrival.

Mercedes, Lark's best friend since second grade, waved excitedly and pointed at the table in front of an empty seat. "I ordered for you. What took you so long?"

"Rough morning," Lark said softly and took her seat. She picked up the cup and sipped the drink and found herself smiling again. S'mores made everything better; including coffee. "Ah! My favorite. Thanks, Sadie."

When Larkin's father was discharged from the Army, they moved to nearby Kohler. Her first day of school, she sat on the sidewalk and cried, too afraid to actually go in. Mercedes found her and let Larkin borrow her favorite *My Little Pony* to get her through the day. Unfortunately, her articulation disorder prevented Lark from being able to call her new best friend by name. The closest she got was 'Sadie' and the nickname took with all the other kids, thankfully. The next year, her father would ensure the kids made her life a living hell anyhow.

"So, you heard then?" Piper asked.

"Heard what?" Larkin sipped and leaned back in the chair letting the coffee-flavored milkshake with hot fudge swirl and mini-marshmallows carry away the image of the cat. "Are they canceling Halloween or something?"

"Linda was murdered last night," Mercedes said softly. "Someone cut her head off."

"Don't overexaggerate," Piper bemoaned. "The report said it was *almost* cut off."

"That's better," Sadie muttered.

"Oh my god! That's not something you just mention over coffee, Piper." Lark pointed at the other three empty seats. "Have you checked on the others?"

"They're fine." Piper flapped her hand in the air. "Mostly. Joy went to visit family in Texas. She doesn't want to spend Halloween in town with a murderer on the loose. Brooklyn and Renee are staying home until they hear from their clients. This might have changed some people's plans, after all."

Lark looked at her incredulously. "Shouldn't we be changing *our* plans?"

"Linda is dead." Piper took a pull off the

vape and blew out a series of rings. "She has a reason to miss work. We don't, bitches."

"They haven't found the killer," Mercedes groaned. "That's a pretty good reason."

"Is it?" Piper leaned her elbow on the table and waited for elaboration that didn't come. "Lark needs jobs to get into that Irish nanny's club. Your mom's been out of work since her surgery and your dad may not have a job if the cops are right about Steve."

"Wait." Lark grabbed Piper's wrist. "What about Steve?"

"I guess people saw Steve and Linda arguing at the movies last night." Piper turned her attention back to Mercedes. "I mean, what if Steve's really a serial killer or something? There could be hundreds of bodies buried in his family's spinach fields. Your dad's not going to be working while the FBI digs the place up. It's Halloween and there's a murderer out there. We can charge triple and people will pay it this weekend."

Larkin's phone buzzed with a text alert. She read it quickly and slid the phone to where Piper could see the screen. "Looks like you get to test that theory. The Mercers want me to come sit tonight."

"See? You got your first regulars." Piper spread her hands over the phone like she'd turned water to wine. "Great omelets start with broken eggs."

"That broken egg was our friend," Mercedes

gasped.

"Not really." Piper crossed her arms. "I barely knew her at all. Hell, I thought her name was Laura until like a month ago."

"Jesus, you are incredible." Lark glared at Piper, ready to say more when her eyes shifted over the blonde's shoulder. "Oh damn."

Steve Fitzhugh gripped the back of Piper's chair. "Hey, girls."

Piper squealed and twisted around to look at the suspected-murderer. "I will fucking pepper spray you."

"Shit." Steve rubbed his face with both hands. "Look, I came to apologize."

"This isn't the kind of thing you just wipe away with 'sorry,' Steve!" Piper reached over the chair and pushed him back.

"It was just fucking candy." Steve grunted. "Why can't girls make any kind of sense? Look, is Linda coming to y'all's meeting today or not?"

"Obviously, not." Mercedes looked at the other two sitters. "Oh, shit. Guys, I don't think he actually knows."

Lark smacked her lips. "Good guess, Sadie."

"What don't I know?" Steve put his hand pack on Piper's chair and knelt down to a more accommodating height. "What happened?"

"You know there's more to the news than just the sports coverage, right? Linda was murdered last night," Piper said matter-of-factly. She patted his head. "And you're the prime suspect, dumbass."

"What?" Steve bolted upright and looked around the strip mall.

People were already staring his direction. He saw them with their phones out—some calling the cops, others recording him, and some obliviously scrolling their social media. Steve watched the police cruiser pull into the parking lot of Game Planet, just three shops down. One of the bistro diners was waving for their attention.

Piper cupped her hands around her mouth. "He's right here!"

"What the fuck, Piper?" Steve huffed.

"You're innocent, aren't you?" She smirked and blew a vape cloud into his face.

Steve took off running and the cops started after him.

Piper shrugged. "Guess he isn't."

"Maybe." Larkin watched the pursuit until the uniforms disappeared around the end of the building. "Seems to be the case around here. Hunter broke into the house I was working last night... and then killed a cat for me."

"Romance isn't dead," Piper mused. "My last date only gave me flowers."

"And gonorrhea," Larkin added. "How is John?"

"It was a yeast infection, you twat." Piper scowled and flipped her off.

"I swear, this town has the shittiest men," Mercedes grumbled. "Like a boyfriend that only cheats on you and calls you fat would be Prince Charming compared to the lunatics we get here."

"What am I going to do?" Larkin asked.

"Go home and get ready to sit for the Mercers," Piper responded. "Keep them happy and they'll get you plenty of jobs. The Mercers know everyone. You'll be so busy, you won't even know the year is up until they're asking for your boarding pass."

"Yeah." Lark leaned back in the chair and turned the cup in her hands, thinking about the night before. "What about Hunter?"

"Hope he finds someone else to stalk," Piper said with a shrug. "If the other girls don't have gigs tonight, maybe one of them can come sit with you for safety."

"Tag team babysitting," Lark scoffed. "Who thought it would come to this?"

Mercedes was clicking her nails on the table again, focusing her stare at a spot of concrete. Her face was tense with concentration as she scrolled through the mental library of true crime facts she collected.

"What is it Sadie?" Lark asked.

"This happened before." Mercedes broke her concentration and looked at the girls. She snapped her fingers as the facts came to her. "The Sauer family! That was them. They lived outside of town like twenty-five years ago."

"Oh shit." Piper rubbed her lip. "My mom told me about that."

"Really?" Larkin sat up. "I've lived here my whole life. You'd think I'd know what you're talking about."

"It's not something they advertise. Mom was in a babysitter's club in high school," Piper continued. "One of the girls worked for the Sauers. She told me all about it when we started our club."

Lark waited for more and then threw a hand into the air when nothing came. "Well?"

"Sorry, thought it was obvious. The girl was banging the dad and when the wife found out she killed them both. Their son, Ryan, saw the whole thing! Aileen lost her shit and committed suicide right there next to the kid." Piper dragged a finger across her throat. "Cut herself ear-to-ear."

"Aileen Sauer," Mercedes whispered the name like a curse. "She didn't kill herself though."

"Yeah, she did." Piper rolled her eyes. "That's what happens when you cut your throat."

"She did cut her throat but the neighbor was an off-duty firefighter." Mercedes looked to both girls, who were equally perplexed, and then sighed. "There's this YouTube series called *Death in a Small Town* that did a whole episode about it. Anyway, when 911 dispatched the call, he heard it and went straight over. He saved her and she got sent to the asylum for the rest of her life."

"Is she still there?" Lark asked.

Mercedes thought about it and pursed her lips. "It was an old episode, so maybe not."

"That's not unsettling at all." Lark collected

her phone, tucked it into her messenger bag, and stood up. "I need to run errands for mom and get ready to sit for the Mercers, I guess. You two be careful."

"You too," Mercedes said softly. "I'll come check on you tonight. I have the Grace kids tonight, but their dad works third shift so I don't need to be there until nine."

"Sounds good." Larkin leaned down to hug her and then walked back to her car.

Standing outside his truck at the far side of the parking lot, Hunter Hogan waved and then made cat claws with his fingers. He was too far away to hear him, but Larkin could see he was laughing. She got in the Camry and started the ignition before taking her phone out. She told Mister Mercer she would take the job and then checked her bank account. She had enough money to make one extra stop while she was out.

CHAPTER
SEVEN

Britt Mercer answered the door more tactfully dressed than on their first encounter. The polo shirt, with its Copper Creek Estates logo embroidered on the breast, stretched across his tightly muscled torso as he leaned on the doorframe.

"I'm glad I could get you to come," he said with that predatory smile of his. "The wife's out of town and I have to go to the office."

"Out of town?" Lark asked with a nod toward Britt's arm which was still barring her entrance. "She didn't say anything about that last night."

Britt moved aside and laughed. "I didn't realize you two got so acquainted. She's normally a moody bitch this time of year."

"Not much for Halloween?" Lark entered the home and set her bag next to the couch.

She examined a framed picture on the end table and picked it up for a closer look. Two children stood on either side of a couple. The little boy, maybe ten or twelve held his father's hand. The girl, a few years younger, clung to her mother's hip. The photo was scratched beneath the glass like a previous frame had broken over it. Dark spots stained its surface sporadically, including one that obscured the mother's face entirely.

"Oh, Erin loves an excuse to dress up." Britt took the picture from Larkin and set it back on the table. "Hard to believe I was such a homely child, isn't it?"

"Luckily the boys take after their mother." Lark smiled. "Will she be gone long?"

"Just through tomorrow night. She went to see her mother for the weekend and should be back Sunday morning. Unfortunately, I have a land deal that's been stagnant until last night and I can't miss my opportunity to make this purchase."

"So much for regular business hours, I guess."

"Regular business hours are for people that don't like making money," he said sharply.

The doorbell rang and Britt spun much too quickly at the surprise.

He went to answer the door and let out a playful growl. "Well, I didn't know Santa still read my letters. Hello, ladies." Britt rested his hands on his hips and looked over his shoulder to Larkin. "Were you expecting friends? Or are they for me?"

Mercedes leaned in the doorway and waved

at Lark. "Hi."

Piper leaned on the door and gave a flick of her hand that might have counted as a wave. "We discussed a safety plan for the club members after you left."

"Oh, yes, that business with Linda," Britt said, covering his mouth with obviously feigned sympathy. "Such a terrible thing to lose someone so young and beautiful. I've been so caught up in my own nonsense I didn't even think to ask how you were holding up, Lark."

She nodded slowly. "Yeah, I'm as good as I can be with it."

"A safety plan does sound like a brilliant idea."

Piper licked her lips and eyed the cut of Mercer's trousers. "I've been told I have a *great head* on my shoulders, sir."

"I'll bet you have." Britt turned his attention to her and held his hands out in front of her chest. "May I have a look?"

"Absolutely," the girl giggled.

"He means at the clipboard, Piper," Mercedes said.

"I know that." She scowled at Mercedes and passed the clipboard to him from under her arm. "It's some simple guidelines like locking the doors and windows, coming up with a safe word for the parents, check-ins with other members of the club, vital places to hit an attacker, and the like. We also included all of our numbers along with those for poison control, a nurse's hotline, and the detective in charge of Linda's murder investigation."

"Oh?" Britt cocked his head toward her. "I heard they had their suspect all wrapped up."

"They still haven't caught Steve," Mercedes informed him. "And they don't have much to go on. He didn't even know Linda was dead when he saw us earlier."

"He came to see you?" He looked back to Larkin. "How scary. Being so close to a murderer, must have been harrowing."

"Alleged murderer," Lark corrected. "I don't think he did it either."

"That's unfortunate." Britt cleared his throat. "I mean, having some closure and knowing it's safe again would be more preferential. I'm going to hang a copy of this on the refrigerator. It really is a brilliant idea."

He took a page and handed the clipboard back to Piper with a sly grin before disappearing into the kitchen.

"Goddamn, girl," Piper whistled softly. "If you end up banging the clients, start with him. Hell, he might even take care of that problem with Hunter. I bet he could handle himself. Did you see the veins in his forearms?"

"Calm your clam, he's a fucking sleaze." Lark waved for one of the safety sheets. "I hate being here with him, but he's fixing to leave."

Mercedes leaned close. "Should we hang out

until he does?"

"No, you're fine." Larkin shook her head. "I want to get some time in with Stone and Branch before bed. They're precious."

"Stone and Branch?" Sadie's stare drifted across the ceiling in thought until she giggled. "Like the houses in *The Three Little Pigs*."

"I didn't catch that." Larkin felt her cheeks warm as she thought about the boys' smiles.

Britt ran his hand across her shoulders as he returned. Lark balled her fist, crumpling the paper within.

"You know," Mister Mercer started. He looked at the girls in turn. "You really can't be safe enough or take too many precautions. I didn't see a car outside. You girl's aren't walking, are you?"

"Well of course." Piper touched his arm. "We got to get in the practice for all that trick-or-treating tomorrow. Unless you want to hire an extra sitter, that is."

"And where would you be sitting?" His lips curled into his wolfish grin and then he pointed outside. "Tonight, I mean. I'll drop you off on my way to the office."

"I'm at the Graces over on Derby," Mercedes said.

"And I'm actually done for the day," Piper added.

"But we do need to take one to Brooklyn," Mercedes added quickly. "She's sitting after all tonight. She's the block before Piper's place though."

"Wonderful," Britt smiled and took his keys from his pocket, clicking the buttons in sequence. The Tesla started in the drive and the doors unlocked. "You girls hop in and I'll be right out."

He hurried upstairs to say goodbye to the boys and then came back down, slipping on his shoes and taking a black hoodie from the coat closet next to the door. He held up a finger and tsked.

"I almost forgot," he said. "I'm just going to sleep at the office since I don't know how long this paperwork will take. It's a bunch of legalese and all, so it won't be quick. There are fresh sheets on the bed in the guest room. Feel free to crash in there whenever you get tired. And do, please, read those safety notes your friends gave you. They could save your life."

He shut the door behind him and Larkin watched the headlights turn away and aim down the street through the beveled glass. When she saw the taillights, she locked up and headed to find the boys. They were the light at the end of the very dark tunnel that had been her entire day.

She found them both in the playroom. Branch was on the bean bag chair while Stone built a fort out of oversized blocks. The littlest looked up and saw her resting against the door. His face split open and he ran to her with his arms wide.

Lark squatted to catch him in a hug. She closed her eyes and squeezed him tight. Then felt

Branch's arms wrap around her neck as well and she tried not to cry. Everything was going to be just fine now.

CHAPTER EIGHT

The first tap on the window did little to get Piper's attention off her phone. Neither did the following six. The next wave came as one vicious battery against the window pane that sounded like a blast of hail. She huffed and slapped the phone down on the pink bedspread before going to investigate. Piper cupped her hands around her eyes and leaned on the window to see what was outside. Another handful of gravel rained against the glass, making her jump.

She slid the window up and lean out to find the pitcher below.

"Knock it off, fucktard!" Piper shouted at the man silhouetted by the street lamp.

"Keep it down," the man responded in a familiar voice. "Can I come up?"

Piper squinted against the glare, cocking her head side-to-side as if it might help her vision. She gasped. "Steve? What are you doing here?"

"Shhh!" He stepped out of the light and

moved closer to the apartment building. "Can I?"

"Why didn't you knock on the door, you dumbass?"

"Because I'm wanted for murder," he hissed. "I can't have anyone see me."

"Then how are you going to get up here?"

Steve pointed at the decorative, vine-laced lattice anchored to the side of every building in Honeysuckle Ridge apartments. Piper leaned out of the second-story window, looked at the decoration and then back to the six-three, former linebacker.

"You're ridiculous," she said with a snort of laughter. "That won't hold you."

"Sure it will." Steve didn't wait for further logical protest and started his ascent.

He wriggled his fingers behind the slats of the wooden squares and hoped for the best. The cross sections were too flat to get footing, leaving his arms and shoulders to do most of the work. Piper watched his slow progress with both amusement and concern. The lattice bent under his weight, but the anchors held tight as he made it past the first-floor window. A board popped and Steve swung from his fingertips, banging against the brickwork. Piper squeaked with nervousness, until he regained control and made it closer to her windowsill. Then Piper felt a different kind of concern.

What if Steve really was the killer?

She disappeared into her bedroom and rummaged through her purse. Piper found what she was looking for and turned in time to see Steve's face appear in the window. She darted forward, arm outstretched and her thumb on the button of the pepper spray dispenser. Steve draped his arms over the sill and pulled himself halfway in with his feet dangling in empty air below.

"Stop right there," Piper growled. "I'll spray you and you'll fall to your death."

Steve's face strained with exertion. "More like fall to a couple broken ribs... but I'd rather not. Please, let me in."

"How do I know you're not the killer?" Her hand shook, her thumb rocking in place on the button.

"Because you know me," he groaned. "I wouldn't kill anyone. I let moths back outside for fuck's sake."

Steve grimaced and slipped slightly.

"Oh, shit." Piper dropped the spray and grabbed his shoulders. "You better not fucking murder me."

Steve heaved himself upward and got the toe of his sneaker against the wall enough to push. They worked together for one final effort that brought him through the window into a heap on the floor. Piper quickly recovered the pepper spray and crawled into the corner, aiming at him.

"Are we really back to this?" he asked, sitting up and resting on the wall.

"Why'd you run from the cops?"

"Because I had an ounce of diesel in my jacket." He shrugged. "I wanted to apologize to Linda. I knew she was pissed about me not getting her candy at the movies, so I was going to smoke her out and take her to buy whatever munchies she wanted."

Piper squinted and let her arm relax. "That's the dumbest thing I've ever heard."

"Killers are supposed to be clever, so that must clear me. Right?"

Piper slid up the wall and sat the spray on the nightstand. "I guess."

Steve got up, head hanging. "If I hadn't fucked up, she wouldn't have been home alone. That makes it my fault, doesn't it?"

"Or you would have both been killed." Piper rubbed his arm. Her fingers traced the line of the muscles. "That would have been waste."

Steve put his hand on her hip with a smile. "I knew you still thought about me."

"Oh, please." Piper rolled her eyes and pushed against his muscular chest. "It was tenth grade."

"And last month," he reminded her. He twisted his fingers in the fabric of her pajama pants and stepped closer.

"I was drunk and you were sweaty," she whined mockingly. "That's like throwing paper in a fire and expecting it not to burn."

"Whatever. You know the sex was always out of this world." Steve's hand slithered across her back and pulled her against him.

"I thought you were here to hide from the cops." Her fingers teased the waistband of his jeans. Then trailed down to the hard bulge waiting below. "Not get in my pants."

"Well, they're not looking for me in there."

His hand moved to Piper's throat, drawing a moan from her. She gripped him through the denim. He was right. The sex was fantastic... for him. The trust fund that accompanied the ten minutes of clumsy thrusting was worth the disappointment. That's why God made batteries, after all. Piper slapped his hand away and kissed his chest, moving down his torso as she sank to her knees.

Have you checked on the kids?

Larkin read the text and sighed.

Of course. It's literally what you're paying me to do, she thought before replying with a simple "yes."

She sank into the couch and closed her eyes. It was all too much. She fumbled for the remote blindly, found it and turned on the TV. A commercial for Hamburger Hamlet was in progress, drawing another sigh. The stupid jingle made her think of her poor mother, slaving at the drive-thru window. Lark needed this job so her mom could quit that greasy cesspool. But the job meant keeping company with judgmental Erin Mercer and her walking hard-on of a husband. She wandered why Linda hadn't warned her about Britt's sleaziness. Then she was thinking about her friend's murder again... and then to her own, if she didn't do something about Hunter.

Life had become a writhing rat king. All its anxieties were twisted together in an insane, diseased knot that pulled her in every direction at once—keeping her stuck in the same spot for all the effort. She pulled her bag to the cushion beside her and found her pill bottle. She dropped two into her palm, absent-mindedly listening to the melodic three-tone alert that the news broadcast had returned from its commercial break.

"We go now to the Moniz Institute for the Criminally Insane with Jennifer Lake, where they've had a very interesting few days. Jennifer, what can you tell us?" The anchorman asked as his face shrank to a tiny square in the corner of the screen.

"That's right, Rex! We're here at the Moniz Institute, where a glitch in the new, automated, security system resulted in an early release for most of the patients." Jennifer, who had recently been promoted from weathergirl and still had all the mannerisms of one, pivoted and swept her hand across the scene. "While the majority of them have been safely returned to their quarters, there are some problematic stragglers."

Behind her was a twenty-foot fence surrounding the institute and a sprawl of browning lawn that was occupied by dozens of inmates gathering into makeshift tribes of lunacy. Some were naked, others wore their issued scrubs, and most were armed. Jennifer gestured to the groups like storm fronts converging on a tiny number of guards in riot gear and wielding dog-catcher poles.

"The patients from the north wing are still resisting faculty efforts after three long days. This is very concerning as these are the patients for the NPR, or No-Probable-Release, ward and include two serial killers and at least one cannibal who can be seen here," the reporter made a circle around one of the patients with her finger. "It is unclear if that is his blood on his face, or if he's found himself a snack."

"Great, that's just what we need. Let's add an escaped mental patient to the Halloween weekend," Lark said. Her eyes focused on a solitary figure wandering along the fence in a Thorazine-induced shuffle.

The elderly lady's robe blew in the fall breeze and her head lulled back in forth to a song only she could here. Lark watched her amble along and muted the TV. She opened the internet on her phone and tried to remember what Piper and Sadie told her earlier.

"Damn, what was the name?" She watched the screen dim as she stared at the keypad trying to remember. "Got it."

She tried the name with a mix of spellings until she got it right. The search results came up with the usual paid ads for background checks and people finding services first, then got to the good stuff. Lark scrolled past the link proclaiming to have the actual crime scene photos and went to a more sanitary write up on the incident—maybe too sanitary as it was essentially the same as Sadie's earlier recounting. Lark took a deep breath and went back a page, clicking on the link for pictures.

It was one of those annoying slideshows that had taken over the internet and Lark considered leaving the site. The first pictures were backstory. There was one of the house, then the sitter's car in the drive, the detectives working the scene. All with their own captions. Next, they got bloody. Just the blood—a pool of it on the carpet below strands of blonde hair dangling from above, arterial spray across shattered glass, spattering on the ceiling that flicked off the murder weapon. Then came an ad for car insurance, the one with that annoying European chameleon. When it ended, the slideshow jumped to the battered face of Stacy Borman without warning.

Lark turned the phone away and tried thinking about puppies, the kids upstairs, that stupid talking chameleon... anything to keep the imagine from burning into her mind. She was sure it was too late. She flipped the phone back over and saw Mister Sauer's bare ass with his legs in the air and a cop bent to examine the wounds. Then came another of an ambulance and a little kid in pajamas being wrapped in a blanket and finally a shot of the sprawling, Moniz Institute for the Criminally Insane.

"Sonofabitch." Lark's mind raced with the possibility that Aileen Sauer might have escaped.

The security failure was the day before Linda's murder. The timing was right. Aileen was the perfect suspect. She probably thought all babysitters were Stacy or something. There was no telling how Aileen Sauer's mind worked after what she'd done. Larkin went to the kitchen and grabbed the safety guidelines Piper made. She started to dial the number listed under 'Detective Brake' and then thought about what Hunter had said the day before. If she looked crazy, no one would ever believe her.

Yes, I was just calling to tell you that I cracked the case and that the killer is Aileen Sauer who's probably sixty by now, Lark thought. *That sounds likely. Not even slightly paranoid. Let's just go with that and see if anyone comes next time I call.*

Lark huffed and went to check on the kids. Stone was already asleep and Branch was playing with his tablet, but it was bobbing and tilting as he tried to fight off exhaustion. Lark left him to it and checked the upstairs windows to ensure they were locked before going downstairs to repeat the process. She pulled each door as she twisted the locks, just to be sure. She started to call Piper and

DAVID O'HANLON

then thought better of it.

Larkin went back to the internet app and searched for the Moniz Institute. On their homepage, she was greeted by a black-and-white photo of a man that could have been the lovechild of Hitler, and Lurch from the Addams Family. She looked around for an inmate listing, hoping it would be as simple as searching the county jail intake. It was not. She went to the contact section and pressed the chain of blue numerals to dial.

"Moniz Institute for Mental Relaxation and Joyful Thoughts," a chirper male voice said. "How may I help you tonight?"

"Oh, ummm," Lark cleared her throat. "Sorry, I thought I'd get voicemail this late and wasn't really prepared to talk to a person."

"I can make a robot voice and say 'beep' if that would put you at ease," he assured her.

Lark pulled the phone from her ear and looked at the website again. "You're not really what I expected."

"Because I'm not a machine?" he sounded dejected. "I wish I could've met your expectations, miss."

"No, no, that's not what I meant." Lark thought for moment, unsure of what to make of the man on the other end of the call. "This is the Moniz Institute for the Criminally Insane, right?"

"It was. I figured we needed a new name since all the insane criminals are currently out of their cells though." He laughed softly.

It was the same kind of laugh Lark's grandpa had before he passed and she felt herself relax a little for the first time in weeks. She sighed and debated hanging up. She didn't want to ruin some old man's night, which probably already sucked, with her paranoid fantasy.

"Can I help you with anything tonight, miss? I sure don't mind just talking to you, if you're just wanting some company. I have quite a lot of experience with therapy. You sound kind of... worried, I suppose." He clicked his tongue. "No, that's not it. You're scared, ain't you?"

"I am," Larkin admitted. "I'm trying to find out about a patient. I need to know if she might have escaped during the... thing, there."

"Oh, so far none of them have managed to get over the fence." He paused. "Well, Jeffery did, but he's harmless. If you live close, I would suggest not leaving any pets outside for the time being however. Jeffery is a real *animal lover*... if you catch my meaning."

Lark's face scrunched and she shivered. "I do. Yeah, that's not what I was worried about. I am now though, so that sucks. I was actually calling about Aileen Sauer."

"Oh," the man said with smile that could be heard. "Aileen got transferred out of here years ago."

"Really?" Lark wasn't sure if she was relieved or more concerned. "Do you know where?"

"I'm afraid I don't. It had a real hippy sounding name, but my memory ain't what it used to be," he said softly. "Aileen barely did move when she was here. She just rocked in her chair and told *The Three Little Pigs* to anyone that would listen. Damn creepy, but harmless. Kind of sweet, in her own semi-catatonic sort of way, even. They sent her to some mental health retreat so they could free up a bed for someone more dangerous here."

"So, she wasn't violent?"

"Oh goodness, no." He laughed again. "I can recite that stupid story word for word, she told me so many times though. She lost her temper that day and her mind, as a result. She wasn't like the rest of the patients. She made a mistake and paid dearly. It's a damn shame the kids had to see the whole thing though. No telling how bad that messed their heads up. Surprised I never seen them come share a room with her, honestly."

"Yeah." Lark's brain focused on the story. Something about *The Three Little Pigs* seemed important. "Thanks for your time, sir."

"Just call me Randolph, miss." He paused again. "Can I have your name, miss?"

"It's Larkin." She didn't know why she told him, but she felt calmer doing so.

"Well, it was a pleasure to talk to you Miss Larkin. If you happen to find Aileen, let her known I said hello, would you?"

"I will. Thanks again." She hung up and sighed.

Larkin went to check the doors and windows again. When she got to the second bay window next to the entertainment center, she sat on the bench and peeked through the blinds. A shadow caught her attention. It was too round, too uniformed. She let the slats slap together and went to get her bag. It bumped the picture, knocking it over.

Larkin picked up the childhood photo of Britt Mercer and studied it for a moment before replacing it.

His tattoo.

Her eyes widened and her heart raced as she remembered the pig poking out over his towel the night before. She looked at the picture again. The little boy and the little girl... and the words of the man on the phone kept echoing back.

Randolph told you something important. Something you heard, but didn't listen to... what was it?

She checked the time on her phone. Sadie was just starting her shift with the Grace kids. She dialed Piper. A text alert went off, but she ignored it as Piper's phone rang until it went to voicemail.

"Shit." She tapped the phone on the edge of the table and then redialed the institute.

CHAPTER NINE

Steve's hand tightened on Piper's throat and she dug her nails into his thigh. His hips slapped against her ass and she rocked back to match his rhythm. He was lasting much longer than usual. Piper bit her lip as her climax built. She owed whoever he'd been fucking a huge thanks for correcting his form. Normally Steve just jackhammered her cervix for six minutes, came, and went to sleep. This time, it was looking like she might get hers too.

"Oh, goddamn it. Yes, yes," she moaned.

Steve's pace quickened and Piper knew she'd fucked up.

"Yeah," he grunted. His angle changed. "You like that? Is that hitting your spot?"

She tried to tell him he wasn't, but his grip tightened, his rhythm broke up... then he shuddered, and stiffened with a high-pitched whine that faded away like Piper's hopes of an orgasm.

She moaned three times, faking one just in case he got exonerated. Circumstances be damned, Steve Fitzhugh was single again—trust fund and all. Her phone lit up and buzzed with an incoming call. It'd been knocked to the floor in the heat of the moment and was too far away to be worth the effort of answering it.

"I told you, the sex is always out of this world." Steve slid out of her and rolled over, pulling one of her decorative pillows under his head. "That took more out of me than running from the cops did."

Piper knew where the conversation was going. She rolled off the edge of the bed and went to the door. "You're not sleeping here."

"Don't be that way, babe." Steve yawned with a dramatic stretch. "I took care of your needs after all."

"Yeah, you sure did." Piper sighed. "I'm going to take a shower. You can nap while I'm in there, but then you're leaving."

"Sounds good," Steve said.

Piper was already gone. The bathroom door slammed and he jumped a little. The phone buzzed on the floor.

"Hey, you forgot your phone in here."

Something tapped the window. Steve looked over and watched. They'd forgotten to close it with everything else going on. Steve snickered. He scooted off the bed and found the phone first then went to the window. Another tap.

"Probably someone pissed about how loud my performance got." He leaned on the sill. "Hey, sorry about that. It just comes with having mad skills."

The phone buzzed in his hand and he looked at the screen. A new text message…

From Linda.

Steve turned away from the window and opened it. He gagged immediately. The picture showed Linda with her throat cut wide. The second gag was more productive, spilling yellow bile across the carpet.

Steve dropped the phone. Something thumped behind him. He turned and the gloved hand hit him in the throat before he could scream. Steve threw a wild punch and the killer ducked under it. The blade plunged into his hip, then slashed the opposite thigh. Steve's hands groped at the gushing wounds. Blood pulsed between his fingers and he slumped to his knees. All his size and strength, canceled with two quick movements. He reached for the killer staring down at him through the cool plastic of the pig mask.

"Moniz Institute for Mental Relaxation and Joyful Thoughts," Randolph answered.

She sighed with relief. She needed answers fast and didn't have time to sit on hold while they found the only person that might have some.

"Hi, Randolph."

"Oh, Miss Larkin, I'm glad you called back." His voice was full of genuine happiness. "I remembered something about that retreat."

"That's great, but I have another question first."

"Yes, what can I do you for?"

"You said 'kids' earlier, but I was told the Sauers only had one kid."

"*They* only had the one," Randolph said. "Howard had another from his first marriage, though."

"There were two kids?" Larkin swallowed hard, staring at the dark stains on the photo. "Thanks for everything, Randolph."

"Oh, don't forget this nugget before you go," he said quickly. "The person that came to get Aileen was from a place called Copper Creek. Told you, it sounds like one of them hippy places. They're probably adjusting her charkas as we speak."

Larkin's head spun and she sank to the couch. "Thank you," she croaked.

"Yes, ma'am. Bet you're glad you didn't get an answering machine now," he joked. "You have a safe Halloween, Miss Larkin."

The line disconnected.

Holy shit, Larkin thought. *Britt Mercer is actually Aileen Sauer's son.*

Larkin got up and paced the living room. She checked outside again and the curious shadow was gone. She sprinted upstairs and looked in on the boys, tucking the blankets around each and stroked their hair in an effort to ground herself in the real world.

It's Arkansas, lots of people have pig tattoos, she thought, picturing the collegiate mascot. *Hell, Mom has one on her ankle. Everyone knows about the Little Pigs. And plenty of people have siblings. You didn't ask about any, so why would he tell you?*

She went to the living room, trying not to hyperventilate as her eyes wandered back to the photograph.

And the stains? Shit, Lark. Things get spilled on photos all the time. This is all paranoia. You're losing your shit. Just like Dad.

She tried the breathing exercises her therapist taught her. They didn't work well when the patient was hyperventilating, however. Lark sank to the floor and slung her bag down beside her. Two more pills and she'd be just fine.

It's all a delusion. You're making up an answer because you're scared shitless of what you don't know and, somehow, working for a murderer is more comforting.

She shook the bottle, spilling tablets into her trembling hands. Lark dropped them onto the table and slid three into her palm, popping them in her mouth and swallowing hard.

What about the name of the company? That's not a delusion.

She tapped the internet app, then the search bar and the microphone icon.

"Copper Creek. Mental Health," she said, shakily, forgoing what would be a wasted attempt at typing.

The phone searched and came up with a number of hits. Her breathing steadied. She scrolled the links and tapped her fingertips to her thumb on her free hand. There was a Copper Creek Asylum just a few hours away in Oklahoma. Copper Creek Healing Center in Texas. Copper Creek Rehab in Kentucky. Another in Oregon. Copper Creek Day Treatment in Michigan.

It was apparently a very popular name.

"Fuck," she sighed, using her sleeve to dry her eyes. "I'm just batshit crazy too."

Lark opened her messages and clicked on the one she sent to Britt Mercer, then pulled down the menu to call him.

"Lark? Is everything alright?" he asked after just one ring.

"Yes," she cleared her throat. "I was getting tired is all. I wanted to make sure you didn't have any last minute changes to your schedule or special instructions before I go to bed."

"That's very good thinking. I like that you plan ahead. Branch was telling me how smart you were and I'm pleased to see he was right. I definitely have the best sitter for the boys," he said. "I hope you know I wouldn't say that if weren't true. Honesty is very important to us."

"Thank you."

"No, thank you. And I don't have any special instructions. Just check up on the boys one last time before hitting the sack please, and do make sure you check out that safety guide your friends

worked on for you. I hope all the other sitters in
your club are staying safe too."

"Me too," she whispered.

"Goodnight, Larkin."

The call ended.

CHAPTER TEN

Piper turned the shower on and dragged open the rickety drawer that always got stuck. It was the safest place to keep her two best friends.

She took out the emergency contraceptive first. Birth control made her gain weight and that just wasn't an acceptable option. Besides, she could always charge Steve for it. Then again, eighteen years of child support from one of the richest families in the state didn't sound bad either. She considered the possibility while rolling the small tab between her fingers. Then she remembered watching the Bingham's one-year-old, squealing shit machine and swallowed the pill without further delay.

She dropped the box in the wastebin beside the toilet and took out her other backup plan for dates gone wrong. The little teal wand buzzed as she turned the knob and leaned her hip on the counter. She teased herself and moaned softly.

"All I need is you and two fresh double-As, little rabbit."

Her thumb adjusted the speed and she tried to stay quieter than the shower. Something clattered in the other room and she groaned. Steve was always so damn clumsy.

"Jesus, are trying fuck up another orgasm?"

She closed her eyes with a huff and focused on her more dire concerns. Steve could afford to buy whatever he broke. And that's where her imagination drifted to as her free hand caressed her breasts. She thought about Steve's rock-hard body and, more importantly, the piles of cash they could fuck on and suddenly he didn't seem so inadequate. Piper pinched a swollen nipple between her fingers, fantasizing about the caress of hundred-dollar bills on her bare ass. And suddenly, she didn't give a damn about how much noise she made.

"Okay, fuckboy. Naptime's over." Piper toweled her hair and leaned on the door.

Steve didn't move. Piper threw the towel at him and got nothing for the effort.

"Goddamn it, Steve. I'm serious." She dropped her robe to the floor and pulled open a dresser drawer for a pair of panties. "You're wanted for murder. You can't just sleep here all night. That would make me an accessory."

She slipped the thong on and snapped the elastic like a guitar string. "Now, maybe, if you wanted to make me something else, it could be justified."

Steve laid motionless and Piper threw her hands in the air.

"You snore like a fucking motorboat so I know you're not asleep." She climbed onto the bed, prowling across it to him. "Is this some sick kink? Being a naughty boy for the hot babysitter?"

Her hand squished on the bedspread and she sat up on her knees. "What the hell did you get on my bed, asshole?" She rubbed her fingers and squinted in the darkness at the warm, black goo oozing across them. The bitter aroma of pennies challenged her stomach's hold on her dinner.

The figure rose from the other side of the bed and Piper fell backwards, knocking her head against the floor. She rolled and scurried away as the killer slashed at her legs, scoring the carpet behind her. Piper got her feet under her and shot forward like a sprinter straight into the living room. She unlocked the deadbolt and threw the door open.

The chain-lock caught and the knob slipped out of her hand. She pulled again to the same result. She screamed in frustrated panic. The knife swiped at her again. Her back burned as the skin parted from shoulder to shoulder. Piper turned and begged feebly before the emotionless, plastic mask. The curved blade of the butcher's knife clanked against the metal door as the fiend lowered the length of the weapon like a paper cutter toward her throat.

Her knee came up into the masked maniac's

groin, drawing a pained groan. The knife made a detour between Piper's breasts, parting meat straight to the ashen bone beneath. The sitter wailed and shoved the killer. She kept her momentum going, angling for the sliding patio door, and crashing through the pane.

She collapsed against the railing.

The killer stalked after her and stopped to examine the jagged shards still clinging to the aluminum frame like broken teeth in a monster's jaw. The murderer nodded in apparent approval and stepped through. Piper beat at her attacker with both fists until the blade cut across her bare belly. She shrieked and pressed herself against the railing.

The black leather fingers curled in her hair and slung her to the patio floor. The knife bit into her thigh and the hands moved up her body, gripping either side of her head and draggin her over the ragged edge of the broken door.

Piper pled for her life. Sobbed. Screamed for anyone to come help her.

The killer shoved her throat onto the translucent fangs. Piper choked and watched her blood spread. The murderer stroked her hair and balled it in their fist... and then twisted Piper's neck until the glass found bone.

Piper's attacker stood up and took Linda's phone out of the hoodie pocket. The camera flashed and then they stomped on the back of Piper's head, severing it from her body.

Another camera flash.

The pills did their job and helped lull Larkin to sleep. As much as she despised the sleaze, talking to Britt Mercer had helped ease her mind some as well. She could hear the staccato clicking of keystrokes in the background of their conversation. He wasn't out doing anything nefarious. He was working, just like he said he would be. Once she convinced herself of her slipping grasp on reality, she felt herself much more at ease. She tried calling Piper one more time and got the voicemail, yet again.

Lark rolled over in her sleep and snored loud enough to wake herself. She smacked her mouth open and closed and watched the lazy oscillation of the ceiling fan through groggy, sleep-filled eyes. The silver slash of moonlight splaying through the edge of the curtains flickered and Lark adjusted her position. Something seemed off by the door—a lump in the otherwise square frame.

She jolted upright, rubbing her eyes with her palms, and found the mystery shape gone and door as it should be. She reached for her bag only to realize it was still dumped over downstairs.

"Fuck," she mouthed and forced herself out of bed to investigate.

A door shut in the hallway and the muscles tensed so tightly in her core, she feared they might break her back. Larkin inched forward, shuffling her feet across the carpet until she was pressed against the jamb and peeking down an abandoned stretch of the hallway. The master bedroom door was wide open and Stone's was slightly ajar, letting the light of the Scooby-Doo lamp cascade through the crack. She lowered herself and eased around the corner to spy the other side of the hall.

A face met her glare and she launched herself backwards, muffling the scream with her shaking hands.

She slid her fingers back into her hair and hung her head with a soft, relieved chuckle.

Stone held his hand to his chest and took heaping gulps of air into his tiny chest. "Good thing I just went pee."

Larkin snorted and laughed as she dropped next to the boy and hugged him. "You sure gave me start, kiddo. What are you doing out of bed?"

"I had a nightmare and needed to go potty," he explained.

"Well, let's get you back in bed and see if we can't think of some nice dreams to have instead." Larkin stood and took his tiny hand in hers.

They walked back to his room and she lifted him into the bed, pulling the covers up and then tucking them under him. Lark sat on the edge of the bed, stroking his hair. He wiggled his arm free from the cocoon of blanket and found her other hand, squeezing her fingers inside his fist.

"There was a monster," he whispered.

"Monsters are super scary."

"Yeah, he had a piggy face but he didn't oink like a cute piggy." Stone sniffled. "He roared like a lion."

Larkin gulped. "A pig monster?"

Stone nodded and squeezed her fingers harder. "That scares you too?"

Lark realized she was trembling. "It does. It sounds super frightening."

"The piggy monster was chasing a pretty girl." He drew his knees to his chest and sniffled again. "He ate her up."

Lark looked down at the boy. Fear's icy fingers slithered up her spine. "I don't think I ever want to have that dream. Let's try to think of something else we can dream about."

"Yeah, that sounds like a good idea." Stone smiled. "Do you think Scoob and the gang would stop the pig monster?"

"They would," she said softly. "Then they'd pull back it's scary mask and we'd see it wasn't a monster at all. It was just some creepy, loser that was weak and bullied other people to get what he wanted."

"Too bad Scoob isn't real." The boy sighed sadly. "But you'll protect me."

"Always." Lark kissed his head. "Think about that until you fall asleep. No more monsters, just you and me and Scooby too."

"Will you sleep in here tonight?" he asked. "I'd feel better if you did."

"I think I would too."

Larkin crawled to the other side of the bed and put an arm around him, nuzzling his hair with her cheek.

"I'll protect you too, Lark," he whispered. "I promise."

CHAPTER ELEVEN

Larkin stretched and returned to the guest room to straighten up the bed. The morning sun cast an appropriate orange glow through the drapes that Halloween morning. Stone was still sound asleep and she made her way to check on Branch. Lark stopped mid-step and turned back to the attic door. She sighed and slid the bar-lock back into position.

"Can't even follow your own rules," she mumbled before going to Branch's door.

She nudged it open and poked her head through the gap. He was out cold with his tablet laying beside him. She snuck into the room and re-covered the device, plugging it in at his desk and rustling his hair on her way out.

Descending the stairs, her nose was de-lighted with the wafting fumes of french toast fry-ing in the kitchen. Britt Mercer turned from the stove to take a sip from the glass on the island. He smiled at Lark and raised the drink in a mock salute.

"Morning. Would you like one? Banana, strawberries, protein isolate, and vodka." He sipped it again. "Breakfast of champions."

"No thanks." She surprised herself with the soft laugh that escaped. "The boys are still sleeping."

Britt checked his Pierre-Arden watch and nodded. "Not surprised. It's only eight-fifteen. They didn't give you any trouble, did they?"

"No, of course not." She rested her elbows on the island. "They're great. Two of the best kids I've ever met, in fact."

"They're very fond of you too." He turned to flip his toast in the skillet. "I'm hosting a Halloween party tonight. I was hoping you'd watch them again. I figure you have plans, but I'll pay triple our agreed rate if you can free yourself up."

"I never have plans," she said. "I would love to spend the time with them."

Again, she surprised herself. She wanted to be away from Britt Mercer. There was still the possibility that he was Linda's killer.

Or the son of the killer.

She thought about questioning him... then she thought about the triple pay he was offering. Hunter was a real, proven threat. If Britt Mercer was a murderer, at least he was a murderer that liked her. In a strange way, that made her feel more comfortable than being at home alone. Halloween was always busy at the hospital. Her mom certainly wouldn't be home.

"Don't they go trick-or-treating?" she asked.

"I'm going to take them to some indoor events early this afternoon."

He dropped the slices on a plate and dipped another into the mixture before tossing it in the pan with a sizzle.

"That sounds fun." Lark thought about her last trick-or-treat outing. "They'll probably enjoy the time with you. It's a shame Missus Mercer is missing out."

"She'd be wet blanket with everything going on," Britt sighed and turned slowly. "There was an incident last night. I don't know the details, but I fear the worse."

Larkin straightened up. "What kind of incident?"

"On the way home this morning, I saw police and ambulances at the Honeysuckle Ridge Apartments," he said.

"Piper's apartments," she gasped.

Britt nodded. "There's six buildings, so maybe it had nothing to do with her."

Lark thought about the unanswered, and unreturned, calls. "Maybe."

"Why don't you bring a friend tonight?" he suggested. "Two kids, two sitters. It makes perfect sense to me. I'll pay her as well, of course."

"If something's happened to Piper, there's not a lot of options left," she said softly. "I'll make some calls and see who's available. I'll come sit with the boys regardless though."

Lark sniffled and checked her phone.

"If you need to talk to someone, I'm not very good at it," Britt admitted. "I understand if you don't want to come tonight."

"I'll be here, Mister Mercer."

Larkin walked into the living room and collected her bag. She opened the front door and looked over her shoulder to see Stone and Branch heading into the kitchen for their breakfast. She smiled and waved even though they didn't see her. She closed the door softly, walking out to her Camry and taking a deep breath of the crisp fall air. Lark let it out slowly in a rolling fog. The dark red pickup idled across the street with the driver asleep behind the wheel and the baseball cap pulled over his face. She didn't need to see him to know it was Hunter snoozing beneath the hat.

Lark got in her car and backed out into the street. She approached the truck slowly while she dug in the console. She let the window down, hanging her hand outside. The spare housekey grated down the side of the pickup as she coasted past it. Larkin smiled contently and sped away.

Mercedes soaked in the bathtub like she did after every overnight gig at the Graces. She never slept when she was working, so she liked to wind down in a scalding, lavender-infused bath and watch her true crime shows until she was ready for bed. She cupped the water in her hand and splashed it over her neck and shoulders and sighed happily while scrolling the list of available episodes with her dry hand.

Death in a Small Town updated sporadically which made it easy to keep up-to-date with, but there were still a few old episodes she hadn't watched. One caught her eye and she sat up briskly, slipping and almost dropping her phone.

"Damn essential oils," she huffed.

Sadie stretched for the towel and wiped the splattered suds off her screen, dried her hands, and then found the episode again. She shivered despite the water being hot enough to turn her skin red. Her thumb hovered over the play icon, unsure she needed the nightmare fuel. She clicked it anyway.

"We're here today, in Ray Falls, Ohio," the host, Gavin Arcane, said in his slow, Louisiana drawl. The camera drew back, showing the burned foundation of a home behind him. "This sleepy burgh was the scene of a grisly series of murders in the fall of 2013."

Sadie's round cheeks floated into a smile as she watched Gavin address the audience. Sure, he was only YouTube famous, but the Cajun mulatto with his storm-gray eyes was her number one celebrity crush. She laid back in the water, listening to him setup the day's tale.

"The incident," he continued, "that we now call, the Babysitter Massacre."

Mercedes quivered at the name again.

The title sequence ran to the spooky, dark-synth theme music and faded back to a drive through tour of Ray Falls before stopping on Gavin Arcane. He sauntered, in the way that only a Cajun boy can, through a perfectly manicured graveyard to a fifteen-foot-tall sculpture of a faceless feminine form sheltering praying children beneath her outstretched arms.

"This memorial was built last summer in honor of the young women who were killed that Halloween," he paused for effect and the lens tightened on his tombstone-hard face, "and those that would perish later."

A text alert startled her and she juggled the phone to keep it from hitting the water. It slapped against her wet breasts and she clutched it tightly to her and tossed her head back with a relieved sigh. Her head thumped against the back of the tub.

"Ow." She turned the phone around and opened the message.

Want to keep me company tonight? Sitting for the Mercers. You're getting paid too, Lark's message asked.

Mercedes wasn't sure what she wanted to do. Staying inside, behind locks and clutching her favorite teddy bear was lingering towards the top of the list, however. She went to her internet app and checked the local news. The most recent post showed emergency vehicles outside a barrier of yellow police tape.

"Another Murder in Kohler: Police advise extreme caution this Halloween," it read.

She squinted at the apartments in the background of the picture and tried to quell the building tears. She returned to Lark's message. The episode continued to play in the background as her fingers hovered above the letters, waiting for her to find the right words.

Pick me up on your way. Going to take a nap first, she typed.

She hit send and another text came through. She wouldn't be sleeping again.

Mercedes squeezed the phone tightly and looked at the alert. She tapped it, pulling up the new message from Linda. She saw the read receipt below the image of her friend's corpse. Whoever had Linda's phone, now knew they had Sadie's undivided attention. Another picture came. Mercedes dropped the phone over the side of the tub and pressed her hands to her face, screaming and crying frantically. The phone blipped again. And again. She covered her ears against the notifications as more pictures showed up.

When the messages stopped, she twisted in the tub, splashing water over the side and grasped the phone. She didn't want to look, but saw anyways as she tried going back to swipe back to the home screen with her wet hands. The screen wouldn't respond and she dropped it again. Piper's severed head sat on a counter, staring at the photographer in the last shot.

Sadie shouted for the phone's voice assistant to dial Larkin. It responded in its peppy, eager-to-please voice. The speaker vibrated with the three rings and the line picked up. Lark never had time to answer.

"Come get me now," Sadie called out, sinking into the corner of the tub, hugging herself tightly and crying.

CHAPTER
TWELVE

Detective Jonas Brake rubbed the back of his neck and watched the Crime Scene Unit worked their forensic voodoo. Doc Telly faithfully narrated his notes into the archaic tape recorder he'd been using since 1987. The crime scene nerds all looked the same—business casual polo shirts and iPads with sensible shoes and professional haircuts. Doc looked like the leader of biker gang with his buzzcut, blue jeans, and tattooed forearms bulging beneath the rolled sleeves of his mechanic's shirt.

"Doc!" Brake billowed as he crossed the room.

"Why do you always yell?" Doc clicked the stop button on his recorder.

"It fills everyone with a sense of urgency," Brake explained.

"It fills me with anxiety."

"I'll keep that in mind." Brake turned his attention to a uniformed officer entering the bedroom. "Goddamn it, Mickle!"

Doc rolled his eyes.

Mickle looked around nervously, stammering for an acceptable apology.

"You are as useful as a cock in a convent," Brake growled. "You're tracking through the blood."

"Sorry, sir." Mickle stepped backwards quickly, leaving bloody footprints in the carpet. "There's just so much of it."

He wasn't wrong. The area between the bed and window was a sea of it with islands of clean carpet spread across the sprawl.

Brake dragged a gloved hand down his face. "Someone mark Sherlock's blunder so we don't get it mixed in with the photos. Doc, break it down for me."

"We found the male victim under the blankets."

"Like he was tucked in?"

"That's an interesting way to put it. I suppose that could be the reasoning. Cause of death was exsanguination. The killer severed the right iliac and left femoral arteries. The cut to the left leg severed part of his penis as well. Tyler bagged it already, if you want to see."

"I'll pass." Brake waved a hand over the boy's body. "There's no signs of a fight. How's someone this big go down so easy?"

"The wounds brought him to the ground."

Doc turned and framed a wide a gory section of the wall with his fingers. Then tracked his imaginary camera down for the detective's benefit.

"You can see how the arterial spray changes height as he fell. I'll need to get an exact measure, but I believe the weapon was perpendicular for the initial attack to the hip."

"Meaning?"

"The perp was crouching. They stabbed him, cut him, and then let him fall. They took away his physical advantages and then went for the coup de grâce, here." Doc tapped the cold flesh below the puncture wound. "A single stab through the jugular notch. I'll confirm when I open him up, but my guess is they went straight to the heart."

"We're looking for a long blade, then?"

"At least seven inches. There's an exit wound in the right buttock where the blade thrusted clean through." Doc shrugged. "It's hunting season, so I'm afraid that's not a great clue."

"Anything else?"

"The killer's small." Doc pointed to a partial footprint on the carpet. "It's only the toe, but I'd say your killer is pretty petite. We'll tear it up and see if there's a better imprint on the carpet pad, but I doubt it."

"Sir?" Mickle cleared his throat.

"You're still here?"

"There's someone outside to see you."

Mickle lifted his heels alternatingly, miming a walk. "They said it's urgent."

"Go on." Doc waved him away. "I still got a lot to do before I leave and I'll have Tyler upload everything for you."

Brake slapped Doc's shoulder and joined Mickle by the door. "Who is it?"

"A witness."

"Why didn't you get me immediately?" Brake grabbed Mickle's arm and started walking, dragging the officer in tow. "Where at?"

Mickle stumbled to keep up. "Bottom of the stairs."

The circus came into view as they descended. Brake scanned the parking lot which was congested with media vehicles, concerned residents, and the tourists there in hopes of seeing a dead body. At the foot of the stairs four officers made a human wall to shield a twitchy lady from the cameras. The woman was in her thirties, but her face said fifties. She picked at a scab on her forearm with the intensity of a game of Operation.

Brake stopped and sized her up. "My name's Detective Brake. This officer tells me you saw something important. Can I get your name?"

"What do you need that for?" She sniffed and rubbed her nose on her shoulder, the way tweakers did when they thought they were being slick. "My name ain't got nothing to do with what I saw?"

"It just makes it easier to address you, that's

all. If you don't tell me your name, I have to make one up for you," Brake said.

"Yeah, fuck it, whatever makes you happy, man. Look I already told Nipple and Putz everything I know, why do I need to repeat it? And why are all these cops so close to me?"

"Mickle and Lutz, ma'am," Mickle corrected her.

"I like her way better actually," Brake grunted. "The officers are making sure no one takes your picture. We have a killer out there and we don't want them knowing anyone saw them. So, the sooner you tell me what you saw, the sooner I can catch this asshole."

"I was up doing... things, man." The lady pranced in place, her fingers going back to the now-bleeding scab. "So, I heard this screaming and I looked outside. I can see that apartment from my living room window, you know, so I was watching because of the screams and I guess they were just fucking or something."

"That's insightful." Brake scowled.

"I saw someone climbing the lattice but I thought it was just like a pervert or whatever. To each their own, you know what I mean, so I wasn't going to kink shame this dude for wanting to climb up the wall and jerk it or whatever. We all got our thing, right? So, I'm thinking this dude just is into weird shit. I like having my nipples shocked, you know what I mean? You too, I mean yeah you got the tie and jacket and look all professional but you got your thing, am I right? Probably something to do with asses. I get that vibe from you. Do you get vibes?"

Brake snapped his fingers repeatedly. "To the point!"

The lady's overly-dilated eyes shot up to him, twitching between his face and the snapping fingers.

"Right," the nosy neighbor said with a nod that didn't want to end and continued through her frantic breakdown of what happened next. "So, the pervert slipped through the window and I ain't really see nothing then because the room was dark and they were wearing a black hoodie."

"Finally, a detail." Brake turned to Mickle. "You think you can remember that one or should we be taking notes?"

"Already wrote it down, sir." Mickle beamed with pride and held up his small, spiral notebook.

"Great." Brake returned his attention to the witness. "Did you see anything else? Or should I just put out the APB for a pervert in a black hoodie?"

"Well there wasn't nothing else for a while so I started cleaning and I was going to have company tonight so I went outside to scrub the patio." The woman looked around nervously. "The girl fell through the door. It broke all to shit and I thought she was just partying way too hard."

Brake's hands pumped open and closed with his growing frustration. "And what really happened?"

"This crazy fucker followed her out and they were fighting. She was screaming for help and then she went down and that's when I saw the knife." The tweaker shrugged. "I ran in and got my phone and called y'all, you know. So, I'm hiding and watching through the blinds and the guy starts taking pictures."

"Pictures?" Brake ran his tongue over his teeth and scowled. "Anything else?"

"Yeah, so the flash from the camera lit him up good and saw him and I about shit myself" the woman said, slipping a phone from her bra. "I tried to get a picture of him, but the camera wouldn't zoom that close."

Brake squinted at it. "You're right, I can't see shit."

"Look at the face, dude." She scratched at herself. "He's wearing a mask."

There was a dab of color visible under the edge of the hood, but Brake couldn't tell what it was. He couldn't even confirm it was a mask at all. He handed her the phone back and wiped his hand on his pantleg.

"Did you get a look at the mask?" Officer Mickle asked.

"It was a pig." The witness nodded excitedly and hugged herself tight. "The guy was wearing a pig mask."

Brake thanked her and walked away with Mickle. "Does anyone else know what she saw?"

"No, sir. Me and Lutz asked for basics and she said she saw someone climbing in the window and then saw the guy chasing the girl onto the patio and I came and got you right away."

"Good. No one needs to know we have a witness and they damn sure don't need to find out that it's some meth addict that was up playing window Nintendo." Brake grabbed Mickle's tie and pulled him close. "And we definitely do not mention the mask!"

"Understood, sir."

Brake released him and started toward his car with Mickle following close. He took out his cellphone and sent a text to his ex-wife to let her know he wouldn't be picking the kids up. She called immediately after it sent. Brake silenced the phone and stuck it back in his pocket.

"This is the kind of shit that made me quit the Bureau," Brake said as much to no one as he did to Mickle. "It's not cops and robbers nowadays. It's psychos in fucking masks with machetes and power tools and goddamn victims in crawlspaces. What's wrong with just being a normal bad guy?"

"So, this isn't a normal bad guy," a woman said as her and the camera man lurched from behind a parked car.

"Goddamn it!" Brake stopped in his tracks. "The press isn't allowed back here."

"I'm Jennifer Lake with Channel Seven, bringing you the news as it happens and I'm here with the detective in charge of this grisly investigation."

"No, you're not because I'm leaving." Brake snapped his fingers at the cameraman. "And you turn that shit off."

"The people have a right to know what's happening," Jennifer said.

"Spare me the 'doing it for the people' act, Miss Lake." Brake slapped Mickle's hand away as the officer tried to reign him in. "I know who you are. You don't give one sugar-frosted shit about the people."

"Excuse me?"

"I said turn it off," Brake told the cameraman again in a tone that got the result he wanted. The little red light blinked off and Brake turned back to Jennifer Lake. "Every news station in a hundred miles wanted someone at that school last year and you were closest. You looked at those dead kids and saw a career opportunity."

"That's preposterous," Lake scoffed. "The shooting was a tragedy and the people needed—no, deserved—to know what was happening."

"Horseshit. You took out your phone and went live and got out from in front of the weather map as a reward. You turned murdered babies into a promotion. So, feel free to fuck right off and get away from crime scene."

"At least tell us you have a lead," Lake whined. "Or should we all just wait for you to save the day? Like Memphis? I know who you are too, Detective Brake."

Brake's mind drifted back to the ritual killings and to the young man he arrested for them. Two more people were killed while Brake patted himself on the back for a job well done. The Bureau wrote it off as a copycat and the kid stayed in prison for nine years before he was finally acquitted. Brake opened his car door and dropped into the seat. He dug in his pocket for the keys.

"Maybe I made a profited off ruined lives." Lake grabbed his door and leaned close. "But how many lives did you actually ruin with shitty police work? Will you arrest the wrong man again or will you just wait for the Babysitter Slayer to go away on his own?

"Great. You've given him a name already. You fucking people, with your sensationalism and your eyes on the movie rights, turn these bastards into celebrities and every sick, degenerate piece of shit sees it and rushes to join the sideshow." He slipped the key in the ignition, "Would you say reporters have more in common with jackals, or cockroaches?"

Mercedes was still crying when Lark picked her up, but after an hour of effort, and four Xanax, she was calm enough to speak again. Lark patted her friend's leg.

"Remember how we always had matching costumes?" she asked.

"Yeah," Sadie whimpered.

"I want to do that for the boys. Mister Mercer said they're going to be Shaggy and Scooby, so I'm doing Daphne."

Sadie sniffled. "We got time to swing by Hallows Evil if you want. I'm sure they have a red wig to go with your dress."

"Now, that's a great idea." Lark smiled at her and touched her cheek. "It's going to be okay, Sadie. They're going to find this guy."

"Sure they are."

The shopping helped distract them. They focused on the kids and strayed from anything that might make them think about the rash of killings. The two of them had coordinated their costumes since their first Halloween together in second grade. Mercedes decided not to let the recent events break tradition and asked the clerk to check for a Velma costume in her size.

"If nothing else, I'm sure we have time to hit some thrift shops for an orange sweater," Lark said.

"I'd rather just get a premade costume." Sadie chewed her lip. "I was watching my show earlier, when I got the pictures."

"Which show?" Lark asked. "Oh. The one with the Cajun guy you like… Gavin Strange."

"Gavin Arcane," she corrected. "And yeah, that one. *Death in a Small Town.*"

"Probably not the best binge-watching choice given the current events, Sadie."

"There was an episode about the current events, Lark."

"Already?"

"Well, not these actual events." Sadie sighed and rubbed her thighs. The medicine was making it hard to focus, which she supposed meant it was working. "Seven years ago, in Ohio, a bunch of babysitters were murdered."

"I'm sure a lot of babysitters get murdered." Lark's face twisted. "I meant for that to sound way more comforting that it did."

"You failed."

"Exceptionally," Lark groaned.

"Seven years before those killings another babysitter was murdered in the same town." Sadie shook her head. "Maybe it's stupid, but that's a pretty big coincidence. The killings always seven years apart and Ohio isn't that far from here."

Lark thought about it for a moment, wondering if there was a real connection. Her fingers found Sadie's in an attempt to calm herself. Both of them jumped as the clerk slapped the counter.

"You're in luck, ladies," he said behind his repainted Mister Spock mask. "I got one Velma left in stock. She's a popular choice for obvious reasons."

The clerk gave a cat call and held the plastic bag up with the costume inside. The packaging showed a young brunette modeling the outfit. The girls exchanged glances, turned to the clerk who gave an apologetic shrug, and then looked to the costume once more. Lark snorted, trying to hold back her laughter before doubling over as it broke free. Sadie ignored the Lark's braying laugh and sputtered her lips. Her shoulders sagged with defeat.

"Story of my life," she whined. "I'll take it."

CHAPTER
THIRTEEN

Stone waved at the trick-or-treaters with his entire body, sending the floppy ears of his Scooby-Doo costume slapping about. Branch, humoring his brother in a green t-shirt and brown trousers, took the bucket of full-sized candy bars onto the porch to dispense the goodies into each child's receptacle.

Lark adjusted her red wig and smiled happily at the brothers. She was glad she thought to call Britt and see what the boys were dressing up as. The long-sleeved purple dress had been hanging in the closet since she chickened out of the date she'd bought it for. Lark wasn't sure why she owned go-go boots, but she figured it was because they were on sale. Whatever they reason, they worked great for the evening and her mom had a green scarf to complete the makeshift costume. Stone was already prancing excitedly when he saw Lark's car pulling into the driveway and he screeched in disbelief when she stepped out as

Daphne.

Mercedes' decision to come as Velma was met with equal satisfaction, despite the costume not being an exact match to her cartoon counterpart. In fact, it was very different. Since the only Velma Dinkley costume left in stock, was in the adult section.

Sadie tugged at the saffron fabric and reminded herself not to move much or risk an indecent exposure charge. She moved her other arm over her exposed midriff, hoping none of the little goblins coming to the door made fun of her muffin top. Sadie blamed her mother for bringing home all the extra churros, conchas, and besos from their bakery every night. She glanced down and managed a smile. The V-neck sweater made breathing difficult, but her tits looked amazing. She turned her attention to the two grade-schoolers and sputtered her lips.

"The one time I dress sexy and the only witnesses are Phineas and Ferb," she whispered over Lark's shoulder.

"You look sexy in everything, sweetie." Lark rubbed Sadie's bare back and laughed. "But you're in danger of getting pneumonia or a spot on a pervert watch list."

"Thanks," she said quietly.

"I saw Mister Mercer get a hoodie out of the closet over here." She went to get it. "I don't think he'll mind it smelling like a hot, twenty-year-old girl."

"Oh? Are you going to wear it first," Sadie sulked.

"Quit that," Larkin said, holding the closet open and moving the garments aside. "Hmm. It's gone. He must have left it at the office when he came home this morning. I'll go upstairs and get you something."

"I'll take her," Branch volunteered. He passed the candy bowl to Lark and smiled dashingly at Sadie with his hand out. "If you don't mind coming with me."

Sadie blushed and let him lead her upstairs.

Lark tried not to giggle and sat on the little stool next to Stone. Kids ran up and down the sidewalks, shrieking at decorations, yelling the phrase of the night, and having a good time despite the town's recent events. A police cruiser crept down the street with its blue lights flashing. The officers waved at the kids and tossed handfuls of candy to the sidewalks.

"Can you do this by yourself?" Stone squeaked.

"I can, but don't you want to help?"

"I have to go potty and this costume is hard to get off."

"Oh." Lark jiggled the dog tag on his collar. "I'll hold down the fort, sweetie. Go do what you got to do."

She snickered as his tail swung wildly in his mad dash to the restroom. She turned back to the porch in time for another group of candy-hunters.

She waved as they approached. Everyone gave their line and held out their buckets, pillowcases, and sacks for their rewards. Lark gave the wolfman a Snickers, the dream-haunting slasher got a Milky Way, two 3 Musketeers found their way to Imperial Stormtroopers, and the Reese's cups were slipped into the blue pumpkin of a Garbage Pail Kid.

Watching the parade of characters, was always Lark's favorite part of Halloween. These weren't just costumes, after all. They were a piece of each child's heart. It was something they loved that they put on display and shared with the world. She made sure to compliment each and every one of them on their choices and whenever she saw something she didn't recognize, she asked them about it just to hear the excitement with which they shared their beloved character.

Two more waves came and the bowl was getting low. Mercedes laughed at the top of the stairs and descended with Branch still clutching her hand at the end of an oversized, orange windbreaker.

"We figured this still kept the spirit of the costume alive," Sadie said. "He's a clever little gentleman."

"Yes, he is." Larkin shook the bowl. "Do we have more candy bars?"

"Sure do," Branch said and sprinted to get the bowl from her before dashing back to the kitchen.

"He asked me out," Mercedes giggled as she got closer to Larkin. "I told him, if he was still interested, and still a gentleman, then I'd take him out when he turned eighteen."

"You're ridiculous," Lark said.

"It was so cute. I didn't want him to feel bad. He was way sweeter than any of the *men* that have asked. Speaking of, what the fuck is this guy's problem?"

The man stood still and silent and the edge of the porch. A pantyhose stretched over his face concealed his gaze while he tinkled the wind-chimes with his fingertips. He stuffed his gloved hands into the pockets of his army surplus coat and took a long stride forward.

"Oh, I didn't hear you come up." Lark spread her hands. "We're out of treats at the moment, but there's more coming."

"I prefer tricks," he growled.

Lark's eyes widened. She didn't get off a warning. Hunter rushed forward and kicked her in the chest, toppling her off the stool. He slammed the door shut and turned the lock. Mercedes jumped on his back and he pivoted, slamming her into the frame of the door. She fell away and Hunter flipped off the porchlight to keep the nosey ghouls away.

Larkin stood and the backs of his knuckles smacked across her cheek, sending her right back down. The candy bowl clattered to the floor, the treats rustling out. Branch ran to Lark's side. Sadie attacked Hunter again. He clamped a hand around her jaw and punched her in the stomach, slinging her into the entryway. Branch charged at him, only to be swatted to the carpet. Hunter kicked the boy like a bothersome puppy.

"Does it hurt, little guy?" Hunter rubbed Branch's head. "Don't act like a man until you can take a punch like one."

Lark pounced into the living room, flipping the end table over and groping for her bag before Hunter could catch her. Her hands disappeared into the satchel. Hunter stomped on the back of her thigh and lifted her by her dress, tossing her to the couch, empty-handed.

"There's a killer on the loose, little bird," he snarled. He slipped the polished hunting knife from its sheath and wiggled it in the air. "You're about to be another victim. All you had to do was just be with me. Was that so much to ask?"

"Yes," Lark rolled off the couch and stood her ground, "because you're a fucking psycho."

"There's definitely one of them running around." He shrugged. "Guess it wasn't Stevie since they found him dead this morning with that little blonde bitch. No leads, no suspects. Just a *fucking psycho* cutting up babysitters. Whoever it is, if they catch him, will just get blamed for you and that little spic friend of yours too."

"You won't get away with it," she hissed.

"How cliché of you," Hunter laughed. "The real killer is fucked. After I carve the brats into jack-o-lanterns, the cops won't even try taking him alive. No one will ever know it was me."

Lark clenched her fists. "You're not hurting them."

"Then stop me, little bird." He swirled the blade in the air. "One way or another."

The stool shattered over his back and he fell to a knee.

"Does it hurt, little guy?" Sadie asked.

Hunter laughed, then roared, and twisted, scooping her onto his shoulder and tossing her into the big screen TV. Sadie groaned and curled into a ball. Hunter pulled the TV down on top of her and turned his attention to Larkin, who used the opportunity to scramble for her bag again. Hunter balled her hair around his fist. The crackling electricity flared brilliantly in the dim, orange and purple mood lighting of the living room and she whirled around, bringing her hand up.

"Aww!" Hunter jerked his head back.

The pantyhose smoked where it melted into his flesh. Lark pressed the stun gun into his side, getting no result through the thick coat. She went for his neck and he pulled her away by her hair. She zapped his exposed wrist until he let go and went back to his face for another attack. Hunter slugged her across the jaw.

He peeled the smoldering garment from his head, leaving strands of melted nylon dangling from his raw skin. "You stupid bitch!"

Hunter picked the device up and pressed the button, watching the lightening crackle between the contacts. He laughed and chucked it through one of the bay windows before kicking Larkin in the ribs.

"A fucking stun gun? Seriously, little bird? You thought that mail order shit would protect you?"

"That's my job," a tiny voice cracked.

"Is everyone in this goddamn house a hero?" Hunter turned and saw Stone in his Scooby outfit with the long, stuffed snout bobbling over his furled brow. "Do you need to be taught the same lesson as your big brother?"

"Stone…" Larkin wheezed. She held her side and got to her knees. "Run. Now!"

"Stones don't move." The boy shook his head. "They don't get out of the way because they're strong."

"Strong?" Hunter knelt in front of him. "Is that what you think you are, pup? Don't look very strong to me. Not at all."

"There's different ways to be strong," Stone said with conviction despite his trembling, miniscule form.

Hunter looked over his shoulder, glaring at Larkin. "That sounds like something you'd teach the boy. Shame he's going to die proving you wrong." He turned back to Stone and gasped.

The six-year-old plunged Hunter's forgotten knife into him with both hands. He bellowed as Stone twisted the blade. Stone let go and shuffled away as Hunter ripped the knife from below his collar bone and fell backwards. Blood spread like flower blossoms across the white expanse of carpet.

Hunter managed to stand and lifted Lark by her hair. "Enough fucking around."

"Agreed," she growled.

The bridge of his nose collapsed in a vermillion explosion. A sharp crack followed as her knuckles kissed his lips, breaking teeth at the gumline. Hunter reeled back and Lark caught his sleeve, hammering him in the face again and again. He dropped the knife to cover himself from the blows and Lark changed direction, pummeling his ribs instead. The sound of the strikes changed from solid *thwacks* to wet, sloppy, crunches and Hunter fell and rolled away in a sobbing fit.

Larkin followed him. She leaned over and swung down with a resounding crack against the side of his skull. Hunter balled up in a fetal position. Lark pounded his kidney until he rolled over and she straddle him, driving home two more shots. His jaw jutted away from his face and the empty sockets oozed blood down his throat. He murmured and screamed for her to stop.

She did. Hesitantly.

Lark took deep, heaving breathes through a tightly clenched smile. Blood dripped from her raised fist, rolling off the polished, brass curves. She opened her hand, dangling the object from her fingers.

"The stun gun came with this complimentary brass paperweight." She stood up and kicked him in the ribs. "Don't act like a man, until you can take a punch like one."

Stone ran over and wrapped himself around her leg, crying. "I told you I'd protect you, Lark."

"And you did a great job, sweetie."

Hunter dragged himself across the floor until he could crawl. Larkin watched him hobbling along in tears. Sadie came up beside her. Hunter opened the door with agonized effort and flopped onto the porch.

"Should we stop him?" she asked between sniffles.

"No." Larkin was stone-faced. "Let him drag his sorry ass around so everyone can see how pathetic he is."

Branch came and put his arms around his brother. "You're way stronger than I am."

"There's different ways to be strong," Stone whispered.

"Take them upstairs," Larkin told Mercedes.

Sadie nodded and took the boys' hands before limping upstairs. Headlights flashed through the open door. Britt Mercer came running inside still wearing his Green Hornet Halloween costume.

"Lark?" He looked around and stopped cold when he saw her. "Oh my God. What happened? Who was that running away?" His head swiveled around the room. "Where are the boys?"

"They're safe." She tucked the brass knuckles into her bra. "I took care of it. That's what babysitters do."

Her phone buzzed on the floor. She wasn't sure when it fell. Britt picked it up and took it to her.

"Are you alright?" he asked.

Lark looked down at herself and straightened the gore-spattered dress, then turned her bruised face to Mister Mercer. "I think it'll wash out."

She tapped the broken screen and saw she had a new message... from Linda. She opened it and dropped the phone, bolting for the stairs.

"What's going—oh fuck." Britt glared at phone on the floor and the bold, black text glowing through the maze of cracks.

Have you checked on the kids?

CHAPTER FOURTEEN

Mercedes stumbled down the stairs into Larkin's arms, holding her stomach tightly. Fat, oozing ribbons of intestine pushed between her hands as she fought to keep them inside. The slippery organs eluded her, spilling down her thighs and across the steps like a grotesque Slinky. Larkin cradled her and lowered them both down gently.

"Help!" she cried.

Britt Mercer froze at the bottom of the staircase, staring at the girls and then passed them. Larkin turned sharply. The figure stood at the top waving with the curved blade that gleamed darkly with Sadie's blood. The pig mask stared down at her emotionlessly, but Larkin knew the maniac behind the disguise was smiling.

"You motherfucker," she spat.

The killer darted away. A door slammed and Larkin climbed over Sadie, muttering apologies and climbing the stairs as quickly as she could.

Branch and Stone were huddled together outside the playroom and pointing at the attic door. Lark ran into it, twisting the knob and pulling back, but it held firm. She beat her fist against it and pressed a foot to the wall, trying to leverage it open. Glass shattered overhead. Someone screamed outside.

Lark slumped to the floor knowing the killer had escaped. Britt ran past her and joined the boys, hugging them tightly. She watched him tending to them and knew she'd been wrong to ever suspected him. She slid down the stairs to Sadie's side.

Her best friend was breathing shallowly with her head lulled over and her eyes staring absently at the ceiling. Lark slid an arm under her neck and stroked her hair, whispering softly to her about all the things they planned as children.

The police stormed into the house with the guns ready and Lark held a bloody finger to her lips, then closed Sadie's eyes one final time.

Larkin leaned on the side of the cop car and watched the paramedics strap down the gurney with Mercedes wrapped snuggly under the sheet. She wiped her nose on her sleeve and jumped at the sudden burst from the other ambulance's siren. It backed out of the driveway, carrying Britt and the boys to the hospital. Branch's ribs were deep purple and the EMTs wanted to have him checked for internal injuries.

Detective Jonas Brake navigated the dumb-founded officers meandering in the yard. His tie hung loose around his neck and he looked as beaten and exhausted as Larkin. He dug the crumpled cigarette pack from his pocket and pulled one out with his teeth, lighting it with ease despite the buffeting wind. Brake rested a hand on the car next to Larkin.

"Run it down for me," he said with a raspy, deep drawl.

"A trick-or-treater forced his way into the house, I beat the shit out of him."

"Any idea who he was?"

Larkin hesitated. Telling the detective about Hunter was too risky. Hunter had people that would lie for him and Larkin had the shadow of her father hanging over her. Sadie's killer was still out there and she didn't need the cops wasting time with her psychotic ex. After the beating she gave him, he wasn't a threat any longer. The maniac in the pig mask was a different story.

She shook her head. "He was wearing a mask. Just some delinquent I'm sure."

"Okay, so your friend got the kids upstairs and then you got a text." Brake took a plastic bag from his pocket with Lark's phone inside. "You checked the message, realized it wasn't your employer and then went to see."

"That's right," Lark said against the pressure of another crying fit.

"You a superhero, Miss Combs?" Brake set the evidence on top of the squad car, blowing smoked away from Larkin.

"I'm just a babysitter."

Brake snorted. "My babysitter can barely make grilled cheese and you fight off thugs and serial killers. Do clients pay extra for that or is it just part of the package?"

"They killed all my friends." Her voice was nearly lost in the winds of the coming storm.

"Not just your friends," the detective corrected. "Renee Miller is missing. The killer seems to be targeting members of your babysitter's club with exclusivity. In fact, the only two, other than yourself, that seem to be left are Brooklyn James and Joy Baker."

"Joy went to visit family."

"I know. The badge says 'detective' for a reason," Brake grumped. "And Brooklyn James is safely in county lockup."

"What?" Larkin barely knew Brooklyn, but that came as a shock. "Why?"

"Apparently she was stealing from her clients and they caught her on one of those stupid teddy bear cameras." Brake shrugged. "Luck doesn't always look the way you think it should and prison beats a casket."

Larkin pushed away from the car and squared up with the detective, flicking the gold-plated badge on his belt. "So, what have you *detected*? I don't see your officers chasing down leads.

Or are you waiting on luck?"

"Listen wise ass, this isn't a TV show." He wiped an early spritz of rain off his cheek and looked up at the dark clouds, blotting out the moon. "Things don't happen fast."

"Then break it down for me," she said mockingly. "What do you know? Because if you don't know shit then I might as well stand in the middle of the fucking street and wait my turn."

"The killer came in through the attic," he started.

"Was no one else available when they handed out those badges?" Lark's face twisted disdainfully. "I told you, I heard the window break after I chased them into the attic. They wouldn't need to break it, if that's how they got in. And I locked the attic this morning."

"The bar-lock on the outside, or the deadbolt?"

"I didn't know there was a deadbolt." Lark watched Brake's eyes.

He was sizing her up, seeing if she'd catch the facts that he was dangling in front of her. She thought about it, and realized she knew exactly what he was getting at. The killer found the bar-lock at the top of the door, in near-darkness, then disappeared into the attic and bolted the door with a lock that you couldn't see from the other side. They broke the correct window to get to the roof where it sloped closest to the neighbor's billowing mimosa tree. The killer had been in the house before.

She had been in the house before. The girl with the crazy daddy. The girl that was still standing when all her friends were dead.

Oh shit. She bit her tongue trying not to scream. *He thinks you're in on it.*

"What are you getting at, Detective?" she asked with a bit more venom than intended.

"The killer knew that attic," he stated simply.

Lark thought about Erin Mercer's stern command to keep the door locked. "What's in the attic?" she asked.

"A sex dungeon." Brake waved a hand in the air. "Swings, a funky round bed, costumes, handcuffs, leather masks and rubber dicks. Pretty much the usual shit people keep in their attics, I suppose. Wouldn't know, honestly. I only have a basement."

"Oh." Lark cocked her head, not sure of what to say.

"There's a lot of video equipment up there too," he added grimly. "Stacks of home movies, most with people other than the Mercers on them it appears. We'll have to go over all of them to know what it really adds up to, I'm afraid. They might be swingers or porn producers or voyeurs, but whatever the case may be, our list of suspects just exploded."

Brake took another pull off his cigarette, desperate for a last blast of nicotine as the fat

BABYSITTER MASSACRE: DADDY'S LITTLE KILLER

raindrops pelted them with growing intensity. He tossed it to the grass and sniffed.

"Go home, lock up. I'm going to send some officers over to keep an eye on you," he grumbled. "Miss Combs, no more hero shit. I've looked at enough dead little girls this week."

Larkin threw her arms around him in a tight hug—and snatched her phone in the process.

"Thank you for everything, Detective." She released him and tucked her hands behind her. "I'm sorry all this is happening and that I'm being such a bitch. I didn't think about how much you have to do."

"No worries, kid. But I got more of it to do, so beat it." He turned to the meandering police officers and shook his head. He raged across the yard, shouting. "Are you turkeys going to stand around in drown in this rain or just track mud all over my goddamn evidence? If you're not working the scene, you're cruising the streets and looking for this nutcase. Get a fucking move on!"

Lark jogged to her car and slipped inside as the spitting clouds opened up in a biblical downpour. She took her phone out of the bag and dialed the Moniz Institute. Aileen Sauer killed that sitter in front of two kids. Two kids she told about *The Three Little Pigs*. Now there was a lunatic killing sitters in a little pig mask. She was starting to think more clearly. Britt Mercer couldn't be Ryan Sauer.

"Come on, Randolph. Pick up the phone. I

need you to tell me I'm right." She listened to the rings carry on until someone finally picked up.

"Moniz Institute for the Criminally Insane," a weary, wheezing female voice answered.

"Fuck." Lark ended the call.

She opened the internet and searched Copper Creek Estates. She found the listing and looked at the address. There was one for the office in downtown Kohler where Britt Mercer worked. And then there was another. The one out in the country where someone could really focus on their art. Lark clicked for directions and backed the car out of the drive. She watched Detective Brake pat his pockets. His shoulders sagged and he watched the car zip away.

CHAPTER FIFTEEN

Larkin was only six months old when her father landed in Afghanistan. She was two by the time he returned, though he didn't come back the same as he left. She was too young to know that though. He went away again and again. Three tours in the War on Terror and the shell of Bobby Combs finally got to come home for good.

Only he didn't come alone.

The doctors called it PTSD, but the malevolent thing that crept into his mind out there in those caves was far more sinister. The paranoia and the anger were too much and Larkin's mom divorced him. He tried the therapy and the pills. He tried being a good father, and for a time he succeeded.

When Larkin was eight, he took her and Mercedes trick-or-treating. The girls went dressed as a cheeseburger and a carton of fries. It was a wonderful night. Everything was absolutely perfect.

And it would be the last memory Larkin got to make with her father.

Bobby and a war buddy went hunting a week later. It's a dangerous time of year in the woods of Arkansas and the two men weren't wearing their orange safety vests. A fifteen-year-old hunter on his first trip out, thought he saw his trophy moving through the trees and fired nervously.

Bobby Combs watched his friend's head burst from the high-powered bullet expanding inside. His mind broke as easily as the one that splattered across his face. The instincts cultivated through four years of warfare came rushing back. He returned fire, killing the enemy sniper.

Bobby prowled the woods for three days, desperately trying to escape the Taliban that pursued him. He tried to hold them off and watched them fall in his scope. When he ran out of bullets, they swarmed in on him. The cops dragged him from the cave, screaming at them in Farsi and swinging his camping ax.

Was Dad already crazy? Or did killing that kid push him over the edge?

Lark drove under the railroad overpass. The wipers worked at full speed to keep the windshield clear in the storm.

What about Aileen? Was she insane before or after she murdered her husband and the babysitter? Where was the line, if there was one at all? Or were they just born crazy?

The lights of the Silver Bells Motel were a

blur through the cascading waterfall. She could just barely hear music and gunshots over the downpour. The deviants of Hell's Bells knew how to party, but not when to stop. Massive bonfires fought the rain for survival and the residents of the shantytown continued their various chemically-induced celebrations. She pictured Hunter crawling back to his trailer to tend his wounds.

What about you? Are you losing it? Did the killings break your grip on reality?

Larkin tried shaking away the thought. It held tight.

Or were you born this way? You're not telling the cops what you know because you're afraid they'll think you're batshit just like Dad.

"No," she answered herself aloud.

Then why are you driving to the country to find the killer yourself?

Lark flipped on the high beams and continued down the ever-darkening road to the old highway cutoff. Her mind drifted to Hunter's mangled face as he begged for her to stop hitting him. Maybe she was crazy. Lark checked the GPS on her phone—seventeen minutes until she arrived at her destination. She felt her bruised facial muscles ache as they tensed into a smile.

"Little pig, little pig, let me in."

CHAPTER SIXTEEN

The Toyota bounced over the hump and rumbled across the truss bridge. Copper Creek was swelling, roiling over the lip of the bridge. If the storm continued much longer, it would be impassable soon. Larkin pressed the accelerator down a little harder. Once she proved her theory, she'd call the cops and hope they got to her before the bridge was underwater.

The GPS told her to turn left, but she couldn't see the concealed, private road until she was passing it. Lark pulled the handbrake and slid the car sideways. She released the brake and cranked the wheel to finish her turn before rolling onto the one-lane path. The crunching of the gravel was drowned in the torrential onslaught from above. If she was right, then Ryan Sauer wouldn't know she was coming.

She flipped off the headlights and let the car crawl along, keeping the needle below the ten mile-per-hour hash. The GPS showed the curves of the twisting path and she used it, and the marginal amount of moonlight, to navigate toward her final destination. The darkness before her gained substance as she drew nearer and she checked the map one more time before switching off the phone. The house was right in front of her, hiding in plain sight.

Lark eased the handbrake on again so the taillights wouldn't give her away and slipped the car into park. She didn't bother shutting it off. She might need to make a hasty retreat. Her fingers curled around the door handle and froze.

"Shit," she whispered, looking up at the interior lighting.

Lark sighed and pressed the button to let the window down. The frigid assault of the rain drew a shocked squeal. She still couldn't see the house except as a vague shadow against the backdrop of night. Lark pulled herself to the windowsill and contorted until she half-fell to her feet. She straightened the purple dress as much as she could, wishing she'd stopped for a change of clothes. Preferably something more functional... and waterproof.

Lark kept low and moved cautiously towards the home. Even up close, the details were hard to see. Then she got a much better view.

The motion-activated floodlight blasted her eyes and she covered her face, blinking futilely to clear the spots from her vision. A shape to her left drew her attention. She remembered it from the crime scene photos—a stone birdbath, now partially concealed by the overgrown weeds pushing through the paving stones. Her boot heels sank in the muck when she tried to run. She dived to the ground and rolled for the shelter of the birdbath.

Oh shit. The car.

She twisted her head over her shoulder in a panic. The spotlight spilled across the yard and she followed the ocean of burning, white illumination with her eyes. Her heart raced faster as she saw more and more of the yard. Then it stopped and she let out a heavy sigh of relief. She'd parked outside the floodlight's reach.

The front door swung open, banging against the wall inside.

Larkin couldn't see the figure clear enough to tell what they were doing. They might have been staring right at her... trying not to laugh as she laid in the mud puddle, hiding behind blades of grass in her violet dress and go-go boots. Her fingers brushed a fragment of stone lost in the pooling water. Lark plucked it free and tossed it quickly at house.

The figure didn't move. Probably didn't even hear the stupid little rock bouncing off the brick wall in the middle of the redneck monsoon. Larkin cursed quietly and tried to remember the layout from the slideshow she watched. There was an attached garage to the left of the front door. That's where the babysitter had parked the day Aileen came home early.

Larkin crawled on her belly toward it, keeping her eyes angled toward the killer standing under the spotlight. Mud slipped down her low neckline like a daring date. She slid her fingers under the door and tried to lift it without any luck. The spotlight clicked off and she could see the glow of lights from inside the home cast through the doorway and onto the front porch. She froze in place and waited for them to disappear again.

The next few seconds passed like days until the spill of light narrowed and finally disappeared. Larkin stood up and tried to lift the garage door with the added leverage. It didn't move, so she shuffled to the next one over.

Yahtzee.

She brought the door up slowly, trying to keep the rattling to a minimum. She bent over, letting it rest on her back as she peered into the void of the garage. The license back bumper of a new Genesis G80 greeted her. She took her phone out of her belt and pressed her palm to the back as she turned on the flashlight. Lark took a deep breath and raised the light.

No one was there. Nothing jumped out at her. She exhaled sharply and set the phone, light-side down on the concrete. She eased herself inside and let the door back in place before collecting her light. The house door was solid. A yellow light flickered in a gap where the weatherstripping had rotted out. She avoided it for a moment and explored the garage as best she could.

Art supplies occupied one entire side of the space. A large easel stood erect on paint-spattered drop clothes next to a short table topped with paints and a fancy, padded stool. Boxes were stacked under and on top of a built-in workbench. Behind it, was a pegboard lined with tools. Larkin walked toward it, her boots clicking noisily in the empty structure. She sat down and slipped them off quickly, then proceeded to the wall of tools.

Her fingers curled around the handle of the weeding tool. She would have preferred a gun, even though she'd never shot one before. It seemed much more intuitive that the miniature pickaxe.

Beggars can't be choosers, Lark.

She held the tool close to her chest and flipped off her flashlight, keeping her eyes focused on the sliver of yellow under the door to guide her in the dark. She tucked the phone into her belt and cocked the mattock back in preparation. Her fingers cruised slowly back and forth until they tapped the handle with a gentle rattle.

It's now or never. You can always run back to the car.

She closed her fist around the knob.

And Ryan Sauer will get away with the whole goddamn thing.

She eased the door open and found herself in the kind of quaint, cozy kitchen she saw in her mom's southern cooking magazines. Maybe it was nerves, but she found herself suddenly reminiscing about her mother's last attempt at one of those recipes. She bit the inside of her cheek to keep from snickering. Lark inched forward, taking tentative steps across the linoleum toward the source of the flickering light. Lark leaned against the archway leading to the living room.

A solitary figure sat in an old fashion rocking chair, teetering placidly before the warmth of the fireplace. Lark scanned the room carefully before moving in and circling the lone occupant.

Aileen Sauer wasn't as old as she expected.

Maybe fifty or fifty-five with a plump, but attractive body draped in a floral nightgown. Ribbons of silver highlighted her thick, auburn hair around her soft, round face. Below that still pretty face ran the long, ugly scar across her throat where she attempted to end her life. The line was thick and ragged, more like a tear than a clean cut. Even though Lark stood directly in front of her, Aileen couldn't see her. She was lost in the same, semi-catatonic fog she'd been in since the murders. Her fingers stroked a plastic Halloween mask in her lap... a little piggy mask.

"Randolph says hi." Lark took her phone out and tapped the emergency call icon. "Guess you'll see him again soon."

"Branch said you were clever," a familiar, feminine voice said from somewhere in the room.

"Not as clever as you." Lark heard the 911

operator answer and she tucked the phone into her belt behind her. "Come on out, Erin."

"Why? Going to hit me with your little garden tool?"

"The thought crossed my mind." Lark tried to guess where Erin Mercer was hiding. "I was actually hoping you'd just turn yourself in."

"You know what they say about hopes, don't you?" Erin said, her voice sounding closer than before.

"I don't. How about you tell me face to face?" Lark squinted at the edges of the room where the firelight didn't reach. She remembered Britt's missing hoodie—the solid black one.

Fuck me.

Erin lunged from the abysmal pool of shadows next to the fireplace. Larkin turned and swung. The flat blade of the weeding hoe swished over the hooded figure. Erin grabbed Lark's arm. Her side burned with pain as the stun gun crackled against her soaking wet skin. Lark buckled and went to the floor. Erin kicked the garden mattock away and held up the stun gun.

"I found this handy little tool lying in my yard earlier," she said playfully. "That was very forward thinking of you. I really wish I could have seen what you did to that lowlife piece of shit that broke into my home... twice."

Lark sniffled and rubbed her scorched shoulder. "He wanted to kill the boys."

"No!" Erin reached behind her. The curved,

twelve-inch blade of the butcher's knife hissed from its nylon sheath. "You stupid little cunt. Take some fucking responsibility!"

"I did. I protected them," Lark muttered. "I saved them!"

Erin spat at her. "They wouldn't have been in danger if you hadn't been there."

"You hired me, you twisted bitch." Larkin sat up. "If you hadn't killed Linda, I would have been out of there after one night. You put me in the house tonight when you murdered my friend."

"You're all the same." Erin circled her. "I told you this filthy profession of yours attracts a certain kind of girl and you're no different. It's never your goddamn fault."

Lark pivoted on her haunches, keeping her eyes locked on the murderous mother and the sweep of German steel waving in her fist. "It wasn't Stacy's fault either," Erin hissed.

"Who?" Lark held up her hand. "You mean your sitter. The one your dad was banging."

Aileen growled from the rocking chair. Her fingers curled into the eye holes of the mask in her lap, but her face never moved. It stayed the same calm, dead thing it had been.

"Lies!" Erin chopped the floor next to Lark's bare feet. "That whore made my father do things to her. She did it! She's the reason he died."

"I'm pretty sure your mom stabbing him in the throat had something to do with it too."

"You filthy bitch." Erin stepped in for another swipe.

Larkin rocked back and kicked Erin's knees. She collapsed next to Lark and the two immediately tangled up. The stun gun clattered across the floor and Lark grabbed Erin's other arm, trying to keep the knife away. Erin punched her in the side and rolled them over so she was on top of the babysitter. Larkin held Erin's right wrist tightly with both hands and pushed the knife back. Erin took the knife with her free hand, leaving Lark control of the empty one.

The killer flipped the knife over and raised it overhead with the tip aimed straight at Lark's face. "Now who's the fucking clever one?"

Still me.

Lark pulled the hand closer and chomped down on Erin's pinky. Dental health was very important to Larkin and her pearly whites grated against the bone until they settled in the joint. She shook her head violently, tearing the digit in half and spitting at Aileen's slippered feet. Lark grabbed Erin's knife hand and shoved it into the fireplace.

Behind the pig mask, the screams intensified until she dropped the knife among the blazing logs. Her glove smoked and caught fire. Erin tore her hand free and rolled away. Aileen growled again, rocking faster in her chair. Larkin got her feet under her and snatched the fireplace poker from its bronze rack.

"Let's hear you squeal like a pig, bitch." Lark

swung the poker and shattered Erin's mask, sending her twirling to the ground. "Come on, Erin. Get up!"

A feral, ear-piercing shriek came from behind and Aileen Sauer jerked Larkin back by her ponytail. She dug her nails into Lark's mud-caked cheeks and pressed her against the wall. Lark slipped a hand between Aileen's arms and stuck her thumb in the woman's eye socket. Aileen twisted away on instinct and howled in pain as she left the orb clutched between Larkin's fingers. The fire poker clanged off the side of her head and she collapsed onto her chair, breaking it to pieces beneath her.

Lark looked at both women laid out before her.

"Shit." She steadied her breathing. "That actually worked out pretty well."

She reached for her phone and found it missing again. She looked around where she'd fallen and found it next to a jagged piece of Aileen's chair. Lark picked it up and held it to her ear. She could hear someone breathing on the other end and keys clicking on a keyboard.

"Are you still there, operator?" she asked.

"I am. Is everything alright, miss?" the operator asked. "What's happened?"

"I just caught the crazy bitch that killed those people in town." She sighed. "Her name is Ryan Sauer."

"We're triangulating your call, but can you

tell us where you are?"

"Yeah, it's a private road. Hold on." She switched to the navigation app to get the name.

Her teeth clamped together as the stun gun bit into the back of her neck. The poker clanked to the floor and she caught herself on the mantle to keep from going down. Another zap of electricity hit her thigh. Lark wailed in agony as it moved up like a zipper, lifting the hem of her skirt in search of more delicate flesh. She let herself fall and curled up on the floor. She shivered and watched the scene unfold.

Erin tore the broken mask away from her swelling face. She shook with rage and pain. Then the second killer put an arm around her and hugged her tightly.

"These fucking whores keep taking and taking," Erin growled. "Look what this little cocktease did to Mother?"

"Well, now you've done it," the man said and stomped on her phone.

Larkin glared at the man hiding behind his cute, but creepy piggy mask. She hated herself. There were three little pigs and she should've known there was someone else working with Aileen and Ryan.

CHAPTER SEVENTEEN

Larkin rolled over on the dusty floor with a hand pressed against the stinging burn running the length of her thigh. The heat of the fire battered her face and cast a glare over the two killers that drew closer to her. She choked back her frustration and pain and scrubbed her tear-filled eyes with her palm.

"Ryan Sauer." Lark groaned and sat up. "That's you, right Erin?"

"Like I said, very clever." Erin nuzzled the man's neck. "I'm done playing with this garbage. It's time to finish it."

He took her wounded hand in his. "I told you, carelessness is costly."

"Why?" Lark cried. "Why did you do all of this?"

"Because you're fucking diseased." Erin grabbed the poker, dragging the point across the floor. "You were trying to force my husband inside you like the dripping, syphilitic cunt that you are!"

"No," Larkin screamed. "You're wrong. I just wanted to be a good sitter."

"A good sitter?" Erin wrung the iron poker in her hands, forcing the nub of her pinky to bleed faster. "A *good sitter* took my daddy away."

"Bullshit." Lark snapped her gaze to the man. "What's your excuse then?"

The gloved hand closed on the pig snout and slid the mask away from his smug face. Britt Mercer tossed the mask into the fireplace and Lark watched it curl and melt and drip across the logs...

And the glowing blade of Erin's knife.

"I don't need any excuses," he said. He squeezed the back of Erin's neck drawing an ecstatic moan. "I just never could stand seeing my baby sister upset. Daddy told me it was my job to keep her safe. Linda hurt her feelings, so I had to kill her."

"He's not always the best husband," Erin said, looking up at Britt's sharp features. "But he has always taken care of me."

Britt turned Erin toward him and kissed her deeply, their tongues slithering across one another. Larkin inched closer to the fireplace. The siblings broke away from their embrace with a strand of saliva twinkling between their lips in the firelight before it fell. Britt raised Erin's injured hand and blew on her ragged stump before kissing it. Erin stroked his cheek.

"You seemed so promising. I really thought

you'd be different than all the rest." Britt turned to Larkin with that predatory grin slashed across his face... until it twisted into something more sinister. "Then you brought that filth into my home."

"Why not just kill Hunter?"

"Who?" Britt's face screwed in confusion. "Oh, not the trailer trash. I meant that scandalous whore, Piper. You brought her there to kill me, the same way Stacy killed our father."

Larkin blinked dumbfoundedly and shook her head. "I keep thinking you can't get any fucking crazier and then you say something like that."

"The stall tactics were cute, but the cops will never get here in time." Britt smirked and checked his watch. "I hope you've got all the answers you need to die happy. I'm going to get Mother to the car. Do whatever makes you happy, my love."

"Put her in mine. The keys are hanging by the door." Erin stalked to Lark's side.

"Yes, my love." Britt heaved Aileen from the floor and over his shoulder. "I'm sure she'll be fine. Nothing a trip to the beach house won't mend."

"The bitch ripped her eye out," Erin hissed. "She'll need more than sunshine, Britt."

"You know what I mean, babe." Britt sighed. "Try to hurry. The creek's getting high and I don't want to have to take the long way around."

"Don't worry, dear. This won't be long." Erin pressed the tip of the fireplace poker into Lark's chest and squatted next to her. "But I'll make sure

149

it feels like it was. Any last words, Lark?"

"Fuck you." Lark turned her head towards the fire and took a series of calming breaths. "And fuck your dead daddy too!"

Her hand shot into the flames, seized the glowing blade from between the logs, and she swung around to bury it between Erin's ribs. They both screamed in pain. Larkin grabbed the hoodie and pulled Erin onto the blade until it wouldn't go any deeper.

Erin toppled backwards. Bits of Lark's skin smoldered on the red-hot steel protruding from her side. Aileen plopped onto the floor while Britt wailed like a wounded beast at the sight of his lover drowning in her own blood. Lark rolled to her feet and darted for the front door. The rapid footfalls giving chase spurred her to move faster. Lark threw open the door. The floodlight kicked on, illuminating the path.

The garden tool whipped past her ear and struck her car with a sharp thwack, embedding into the hood. Lark veered away and into the woods. She'd never get the car in gear and moving before Britt Mercer got his hands on her. She had to keep running.

Rocks and sticks beneath the fallen autumn leaved cut into her bare soles as she slipped into the void of the surrounding forest. She slowed to a jog, keeping her hands in front of her to stop her from crashing into a tree. It seemed to be working. Her palms struck the rough trunk of a pine and she changed her path to go around it.

Between the cloud coverage and the rain, she couldn't see more than a yard. Her ankle clipped a large stone protruding from the ground. She hopped along, trying to stay upright before tumbling down a hill. She cried out as the rocky slope battered her all the way to the bottom. The downpour was loud, but Lark was sure it wasn't as loud as her unintentional descent.

Lark rolled onto her face. An unpleasant knot gouged her left breast as she dragged herself through the leaves and she reached a hand between soaking flesh and the saturated padding to find the source. A burst of elated laughter escaped her lips. She couldn't believe she hadn't lost them in the fight.

Luck doesn't always look the way you think it should, she remembered.

She slipped the brass knuckles over her fingers and slunk behind a nearby tree stump... making as much noise as possible in the process.

The flashlight beam speared overhead and panned methodically. Lark watched it bobbing closer to the hill, angle down to explore the area she'd landed, and then turn away. She rolled her eyes and ground her raw hand against the bark to draw out a scream. The light snapped back around and descended to a soundtrack of obscenities as Britt slide along the rocky path. He stalked through the leaves, between the trees, keeping the light turning in tandem with his gaze. Lark stayed low, half-crawling in a circle to get behind him.

"Come out, Larkin," he shouted, knowing the light was giving him away anyhow. "You don't really think I just started killing people on Thursday, do you? You're not the first prey I've hunted in these woods. You can't outlast me and you're not escaping."

"How's the wife?"

Britt whirled around, straight into the left hook. He stumbled, but didn't fall. He grabbed her around the waist as much for balance as to restrain her. She dug her nails into his face and raked down across his eyes, then hammered him in the ear with brass knuckles. That time he fell.

Britt blinded her with the flashlight and kicked her feet out from under her. He groaned, clamoring to a languid stance. He wiped the blood away from his eyes. A hiss of pain slipped as his fingers found the deep furrow left by the knuckle-duster.

"I should have remembered you had those fucking things," he growled.

She climbed to her feet and held her fists up for another round. "I bet you don't forget next time."

"There won't be a next time, Lark. You're going to die right now." He spat to the side and flipped open a pocket knife. "Just lay down and take it."

"Is that what your sister would do before I killed her?"

"I'm going to cut you from one set of lips to the other, you little bitch." He flashed her with the light again and pounced forward.

Larkin's punch whizzed harmlessly over Britt's head and the knife punched into her side. He dropped the flashlight to grab her hair. The steel edge settled onto her throat.

"You see, Larkin?" Britt pulled her against him. His erection swelled against her in anticipation of the kill. "You put up a great fight, but you're not special. You're just like all the others and you can't stop me… just like they couldn't."

Larkin leaned against him and gently caressed the straining bulge pressing into her thigh. "I get it now," she whispered.

"Get what?"

"The real reason you want to kill me so bad." She laughed. "I stuck more inches in your wife than you even got."

Her hand shifted, squeezing his balls against her blistered palm while her head swung into his nose. Lark felt a pop and Britt's roar became a squeal. She elbowed him in the chest and planted the brass knuckles straight into his throat. He collapsed into a heap, alternating between choking and high-pitched, croaked profanities. Lark found the flashlight and shined it into his face.

"You were right," she said. "Piper's safety notes were full of great tips."

She ran as fast as she could, scurrying up the hill and through the woods. Britt Mercer's furious howling grew increasingly distant. The nightmare was almost over. The thought drove her on despite her pain and exhaustion. The Toyota Camry appeared at the end of the light's reach. Its exhaust drifted through the sheets of rain. It was still running exactly as she'd left it.

Larkin paused as she reached for the doorhandle. She shined the light into the backseat and found it empty. A breath she didn't know she was holding escaped in a massive sigh and she sank into the safety of the car. The cloth seat squished under her.

"That's just how I expected this night to end." She slammed the door and turned on the headlights. "I guess it's not over after all."

Erin Mercer stumbled out of the house. The butcher's knife still stuck out of her side and she braced herself against the brick wall. Her body racked with a coughing fit. She slumped to her knees and looked up at Larkin's car. Her mouth hung agape, spilling blood from her lips like a demented fountain.

"I'll huff," Lark said, placing her hand on the gearshift, "and I'll puff." She slipped it into drive, "and I'll blow your house down!"

Larkin mashed the accelerator to the floor. The tires spun, spewing gravel and mud behind her as the car jumped forward. Erin's face contorted in a spiteful, silent scream. Larkin pulled her seatbelt on quickly, keeping the car aimed straight ahead. The birdbath clipped the mirror, showering her with shrapnel.

She didn't care.

She gripped the wheel tighter and let out a wolf's howl. Erin's face bounced off the hood and the car kept going, slamming her into the brick house and crashing through the living room. The airbag exploded in Larkin's face. Her foot came off the pedal. She watched the fireplace streak by. The car plowed through another wall before she could hit the brakes. The door wouldn't open, so she slid out the window for the second time that night.

Lark limped around the front of the car and found Erin Mercer still clinging to the crumpled bumper, her head impaled on the garden tool like a hood ornament. Her torso had burst like a biscuit can, leaving a path of blood and viscera through the house. Bones stuck through body parts they didn't belong to and the knife was still exactly where Larkin left it. She bent and tore the blade through the side of the mangled body... just in case.

"I quit."

She wandered through the house and found Aileen rocking on the floor holding the last piggy mask once again. Lark raised the knife and paused. Aileen's empty eye socket dripped down her cheek, but she didn't seem to mind. The excitement was over and she was content right where she was, so that's where Larkin left her. Erin's keys were hanging by the garage door, like she'd said.

Lark pulled the garage door up and got

behind the steering wheel of the Genesis sedan, tossing the knife in the passenger seat. She started the car, turned the heater up and backed out. She pulled away from the Sauer death house and onto the private road. The storm was washing out the gravel, making the ride a long, bumpy one. She jostled in the heated seat and sped through the beating.

Then the headlights shined into her rearview.

CHAPTER EIGHTEEN

Once they were back on pavement, the Tesla closed the distance quickly. It banged against her rear bumper. The Genesis swerved on the wet road, but Lark got it straight again. He raced closer. She pumped the brake, letting him hit her earlier than he expected. His car skidded and twisted, giving her a lead again. She pressed the pedal down harder. A moment later, Britt rammed her again.

"Fuck!"

Lark watched him maneuver in her side mirror and try to pull alongside her. Her mind raced for anything that might be useful, but all that she could think about were years of *Mario Kart* and bumper cars at the county fair. Lark's head bounced off the window as he broadsided her, snapping her back into the present. The Tesla veered into the other lane, pulling away for a more powerful blow. She watched as the black sedan whipped toward her.

Larkin mashed the brake, letting Britt zip passed her and off the shoulder. Her foot switched back to the gas and she sped toward the truss bridge in the distance. Britt's car tore through low hanging branches and kicked up rooster tails of mud as he fought the wheel to get back on the road. She watched the car, nothing but a silhouette, regain traction. The attempts to run her off the road had left its headlights smashed out.

Larkin took the bend in the road at sixty. The tires started to slide and an idea came to her. She eased back on the gas enough for Britt to get on her bumper again.

You might die, even if this works. Then again, you're going to die for sure if you don't do something.

Britt moved in for another try. Larkin angled the car gently, careful not to arouse suspicion. She gave it a little more gas and Britt kept pace. The needle passed sixty again and she pulled the handbrake and jerked the wheel to the left, throwing the Genesis into a slide. Britt shot passed her, plowing into the iron uprights of the bridge's frame. Larkin didn't get a chance to celebrate.

Her tires struck the hump where the bridge met the road and sent her car rolling across the bridge until it came to a stop on its roof in a twisted wreck against the opposite side of the structure. She was still strapped to her seat but the roof was bent in so much that her ear was resting on her shoulder. She undid her seatbelt, slumping over. Lark laid there staring out the missing windshield. The creek had risen and was spilling in around her.

This is becoming a fucking habit, she thought while crawling out another car window.

Britt spilled out of his own wreckage. He tried to stand, only to fall flat. He repeated the process four more times before he got it right. Larkin made slow progress across the bridge. Police lights flashed on the old highway, heading toward the scene. Lark had bought them enough time to track her phone, after all. Britt watched their approach and propped himself up

"I guess this is where it gets interesting. Your word against mine." He smiled that wicked smile of his. "And you're the one holding a murder weapon."

"Yeah, I am." Larkin lifted the butcher's knife, looking at the bloody, warped blade she'd killed Erin Mercer with. "You should take it."

Lark thrust the knife between his teeth before he could scream, punching it through the back of his skull and forcing him off the bridge. His body disappeared in a splash, bobbed to the surface, and then floated out of side in the raging current of the rising creek. Lark splashed awkwardly towards the approaching police.

She scraped her hair away from her face and hit the water with a splash. The creek turned to a river, its waters churning noisily around her. She was no stone. The water carried her across the bridge to the submerged railing. A hand gripped her arm and she knew Britt had somehow survived... somehow swam against the current to seize her. She felt the fingers slipping down her arm. A second set of hands found her and she was upright once more.

Lark didn't want to look. She wriggled with what energy she had left.

"I thought I told you to shit-can the heroics," a gruff, growling drawl said.

Larkin managed an amused grunt and opened her eyes, letting Detective Brake guide her to the safety of the nearest police car. He helped her into the back of the car and shook his head.

"Do I want to fucking know?" he asked.

"The Mercers were the killers," Lark whispered. She nodded slowly and cleared her throat, making eye contact. "It was both of them, working together."

"Both of them?" He scratched at his head, raising an eyebrow. "No shit?"

"I thought you'd figure it out. Your badge says 'detective' for a reason."

Brake grunted. "Yeah, no one else was available when they were handing them out."

Lark managed a weak smile. "I killed Erin Mercer. You'll find her body in the house up the way along with an escaped mental patient."

"Escaped mental patient?" Brake loosened his tie and slipped it over his head. "I swear, this job's going to make me hang myself with the damn thing eventually."

"Hope not." Lark looked around at the other cops shining lights at the water, looking for the body of Britt Mercer. "I stabbed him, but he fell in before I could make sure he was dead."

"We'll deal with that later."

"How are the boys?" she asked softly, trying not to cry with the thought of how they'd feel finding out their parents were murdered by the babysitter.

"Resting. I'll get the shit duty and have to tell them their parents are dead. I fucking hate that part. Better than the other way around though." Brake leaned on the door. "We found Renee Miller. She's alive. I don't know how much better that makes you feel, if it does at all, but I thought you might like to know."

"I appreciate that." Lark laced her fingers together and puffed her cheeks before exhaling noisily. "So, is this the part where you arrest me?"

"Thought about it." He shrugged. "Then again, my babysitter sucks and I figured you've got an open schedule since you just killed your last employer."

"You'd think that'd be a deal breaker."

"You'd think." He waved for her to put her legs inside. "You can start on Monday."

Detective Brake shut the door and got behind the wheel, turning the car around on the narrow road. He hit the sirens and aimed toward town. Lark leaned her head against the window, curling her legs into the hard, plastic seat and stretching out as best she could in the confines of the squad car. It wasn't easy, or comfortable, but she didn't mind. She closed her eyes.

And, for a change, sleep came easily for her.

EPILOGUE

Aileen Sauer sat in her rocking chair, teetering placidly. She stroked the soft head of the stuffed pig in her lap and smiled gently at the patients seated on the floor in front of her.

"Howdy, Miss Aileen," a jolly voice said behind her. "We sure have missed you."

The scrawny old man gave her a hug.

"Randolph, my sweet boy." Aileen's voice was raspy and harsh, but still carried that soft, loving maternal tone. She stroked his cheek. "I missed you too. I missed all of you so very much, but you most of all."

Randolph and pulled his hospital-issued robe around his pajamas with a flash of his bright smile. He joined the others and crossed his legs under himself.

"Are you going to tell us our story now, Miss Aileen?" he asked.

Aileen's fingers circled the edge of her eye patch. "I have a new one today, Randolph."

The group of patients murmured amongst themselves in excitement and confusion. It was always *The Three Little Pigs*. It didn't change. Meds at three, dinner at five, and *Three Little Pigs* at six-thirty—every day for the last twenty-four years. Randolph scooted forward.

"A new story?" he asked, full of nervous energy.

"Yes, my lovely boy. Today, I want to tell you all about a very bad wolf that ate up the little piggies." She leaned forward, wringing the stuffed animal in her fists. "And how one old sow is going to rip that pup open and save her babies."

The crowd of lunatics cheered... and Aileen began her tale.

"It's been five weeks since Britt Mercer went missing," Gavin Arcane said, "and the police still have no clues where the killer could be hiding. A video library found in their attic, ties many prominent members of the community to a sex cult ran by the incestuous Mercers. Leading many to believe the surviving half of the Kohler Babysitter Slayers might have had help in fleeing the area, and possibly the country."

Hunter Ray Hogan dropped the phone on the stained mattress beside him and crushed another OxyContin into dust. He lifted the notebook and scraped the powder into his travel mug, pressing the straw between his lips and slurping the painkiller between the wiring holding his jaw shut.

"Searches of the Mercer properties have revealed several stashes of human remains," Gavin continued. "The local police have been flooded with requests to view these remains in connection with open missing persons cases from across the region. The number of bodies found has many wondering, however, if the Mercer Sex Cult found their thrills… with kills."

"That's crazy, don't you think?" Larkin said, her voice was barely above a whisper.

Hunter spat out his drink and looked around the darkness nervously. He squinted at the figure lurking in the graffitied hall of his trailer. He asked who was there in a jumble of syllables that made little sense. Then he grunted two more words that were slightly more recognizable.

"Little bird?"

Larkin stepped out the shadows and stood next to him. His mattress rested straight on the floor, leaving him staring up at her. She reached down and patted his head like a dog.

"Poor, pitiful Hunter," she said. "You were always such a terrible listener. The show you're watching, *Death in a Small Town*, that was Mercedes favorite. It's a good show… very informative. You should pay more attention to what they're telling you."

He broke into inarticulate grumbling again.

"Oh, we are *way* past apologies. Did you hear what Gavin Arcane was saying just now? It's really something else. After everything the town has been through, now they're saying that there's a psycho killer cult on the loose in Kohler." Larkin swung the hatchet from behind her back. "And you're about to become its next victim."

The End

Find More At Babysittermassacre.com

Printed in Great Britain
by Amazon

14085797R00102